BIG PICTURES

stories rare and new by a galaxy of
Ireland's best-known writers for
young people

GW00779025

New writing from thirteen well-known writers, illustrations from two of the country's foremost illustrators - *Big Pictures* is the anthology of the season. Edited by the 1998 winner of the Bisto Book of the Year Award, and with almost two hundred pages of unpublished work from bestsellers and multi-award-winners, it has something for everyone.

About the cover artist:

PJ Lynch *is one of Ireland's most distinguished illus-trators. Since winning the Mother Goose Prize in 1986 he has gone on to collect a clutch of national and inter-national awards. His work on* The Christmas Miracle of Jonathan Toomey *won the Bisto Book of the Year Award, the Reading Association of Ireland Award, and the Kate Greenaway Medal. In 1998* When Jessie Came Over the Sea *won a Bisto Merit Award and the Kate Greenaway Medal (again).*

BIG PICTURES

edited by Gerard Whelan

LETS Dublin

First published 1998 by Lucan Educate Together
School

Front cover illustration by PJ Lynch from *Oscar Wilde:
Stories for Children*, reproduced by permission of the pub-
lisher, MacDonald Young Books. We are especially grate-
ful to both.

British Library Cataloguing in Publication Data. A cata-
logue record for this book is available from the British
Library.

ISBN: 0 9533815 0 1

Typesetting: Claire Ranson
Design: Claire Ranson and Gerard Whelan
Cover design: NPP
Printing and Binding: Colour Books Ltd

All proceeds from the sale of this book will go to Lucan
Educate Together School (LETS), a registered charity.
LETS is the Patron of Lucan Educate Together National
School.

Contents

Robert Dunbar lectures in English at the Church of Ireland College of Education, Rathmines. He was twice president of the Children's Literature Association of Ireland, and a member of the Irish Children's Book Trust. He is a prolific writer and broadcaster on children's literature, a respected editor of anthologies and periodicals, and is widely regarded as Ireland's foremost academic authority in the field. He is probably best known to the general public as 'your man with the Northern accent who does the Christmas feature on kids' books for Gay Byrne's radio show.' Because of his appearance, small children sometimes mistake him for Santa Claus; because of his boundless support for what they try to do, some writers and illustrators tend to agree.

PREFACE

I am very pleased indeed to provide a brief preface for this collection of new Irish writing for the young.

Lucan Educate Together School, which will benefit financially from the book, deserves every possible support. But even if this were not the case, the volume would have many claims to our attention. The writing, in terms of both theme and style, covers a remarkable range: there are contemporary stories and stories set in the past; there is good humour and high seriousness; there are items which will comfort and items which will challenge. It all adds up to a rich, invigorating and enjoyable anthology, one which clearly reflects the originality and imagination of those of today's Irish writers who cater for a youthful audience.

It is a further tribute to these writers that they should have contributed so generously to this project. Educational and literary enterprise have combined in a most laudable act of co-operation. It is one which should have the enthusiastic endorsement of all of us who feel that at the heart of the process generally known as 'education' should be a belief that it is within our school and classroom capability to ensure that the next generation will, somehow, be wiser and happier than ours. To translate this aspiration into reality requires on the part of all of us the kind of imaginative leap which characterises artistic, including literary, endeavour of any worthwhile quality. Peruse the pages which follow and see the possibilities!

Robert Dunbar

INTRODUCTION

The actual aim of this book is to raise funds for Lucan Educate Together School (LETS). I had the notion of doing this by putting together an anthology of stories by many of Ireland's best-known writers for young people, a book that (I hoped) would succeed on its own terms as a collection of stories. Whether or not I've succeeded in doing that is something for you, the reader, to decide.

I feel a bit of a fake calling myself 'editor' of this collection. Apart from the odd bit of foostering here and there, the 'editing' process consisted of trying to arrange the stories in some order that would flow. My main work lay in gathering the stories in the first place, and my fingers did more walking on a phone than a keyboard. But calling yourself 'compiler' or 'arranger' sounds weird, so I'm stuck with being the editor.

To anyone familiar with modern Irish writing for young people, the list of contributors will say more about this book than I could ever do. There are stories and illustrations here from some of the most highly-regarded workers in the field, freely given and in some cases specifically done in support of this project. I asked them for some token thing, and they gave of their best: that's a fine thing to say about anybody.

Only one of these stories has been published before, and that one - Morgan Llywelyn's *Fletcher Found* - is now impossible to lay hands on except in this volume. The sheer range of the material is, it seems to me, a happy indication of the health of Irish writing for the young at the butt-end of the century. The fact that so many noted writers were pleased to join a project of this kind, supporting an educational tradition that positively *celebrates* difference, seems a sign of another kind of health — a good sign in an Ireland where, lately, you would sometimes worry. But then maybe writers are more open to such notions of tolerance and difference as Educate Together embodies: maybe it goes with the territory — if there were no differences, after all, writers would have nothing much to write about.

Special thanks to Larry O'Loughlin and Claire Ranson, whose help and support went far beyond anything I could ask. The book would not exist without them, or without the LETS book committee — Ria Ziere, Martin O'Dowd and Moira O'Flaherty. Naturally this is also true of all the writers and illustrators involved. Their generosity was in many cases overwhelming. My sincerest thanks are due to each and every one of them, and are hereby given.

Gerard Whelan

THE STORIES

Carolyn Swift *is a national treasure. While younger readers continue to enjoy her many novels, older generations know her both as a woman who gave Brendan Behan his start in the theatre and as writer of the t.v. series* Wanderly Wagon. *There isn't room in the book to cover her other achievements — it would take something the size of a phone book even to list them. She is - as this might indicate - a bit of an all rounder.* The Big Picture *is an unpublished story.*

THE BIG PICTURE

by Carolyn Swift

'Hey! You!' Bridget tried to look as if she thought the words were meant for somebody else. Though she could feel her heart pounding, she continued to walk steadily towards the door of the disco, hoping that Molly would follow. Then a heavy hand fell on her shoulder.

Bridget's cheeks burned with a mixture of anger and shame. She had spent ages combing her red hair so it no longer straggled over her shoulders, but looked more like the latest style worn by the young people from the housing estate across the road from the halting site. She had even brushed Molly's stubborn black curls into a pony-tail, warning her not to talk while they waited to pay in on the door, in case their speech might give them away. No-one in the queue had taken much notice of the two girls standing silently among them, and Bridget had begun to believe that their disguise was perfect. Now all her confidence left her as she turned to face the burly man still gripping her right shoulder.

'Yes, you!' the man continued, pulling her roughly out of the queue. 'Both of you! We don't want any of your sort here.'

In her anger, Bridget forgot to watch how she spoke.

'I done nothing, Mister!' she shouted defiantly.

No sooner were the words out of her mouth than she knew she'd given herself away completely.

'We got the money, Mister!' Bridget heard Molly pleading and saw her younger sister's brown eyes staring up at the bouncer with the fixed look which never failed to coax a few pennies from the settled people when she was a toddler, begging on the street. But it had no effect on the bouncer now.

'I don't care what you've got. You're not coming in here. You bloody tinkers are nothing but trouble. Be off with you now.'

Conscious of the stares of other young people in the queue, Bridget grabbed Molly by the arm.

'Come on,' she muttered. 'We're not going to get in here.'

'Will we go over to the chipper?' Molly suggested, as they hurried off down the street, away from the scornful looks and the half-heard jeers. But Bridget shook her head.

'Paddy said there was a traveller from out some place beyond Palmerstown got into a fight there Saturday,' she told her, 'and they put all the travellers out. There's none let into the place since.'

'Why do the settled people put all the travellers down as one?' Molly cried in despair. 'If a fella from Cork or Kerry gets into a fight they don't put everyone from Cork or Kerry out of it!'

Bridget pulled Molly along impatiently.

'Travellers always get hassle. You know that. You was only a babby when we used to go travelling, staying on the sides of the road and fields and that, before we went into the halting site in Coolock. But we was always being put going. If it wasn't the people who owned the land it was the guards, saying we were gathering dirt and that.'

'I'd have told them straight up to give us a skip,' Molly cried. 'We'd put the rubbish in it as good as the settled people if we'd have had one.'

'They wouldn't listen,' Bridget told her irritably. 'And you'd only have to go, because if you didn't the guards would drag you out of it. Make you leave even if it was twelve or one o'clock of a winter's night.'

'I don't know why the guards are so mean to travellers,' Molly said, as they reached the bus stop.

'Ah, you get bad guards and you get good guards,' Bridget shrugged, 'and when they're bad it's mostly the settled people that's put them up to it. But if we'd only be let stay a couple of days here and a couple of days there, until we wanted to move on ourselves, I'd like to go travelling again at this time of the year, when the days are a good length. You get to meet up with different travellers. Not just be always around your own on the site. And we'd have a bit of crack. It wouldn't be so bad not getting into discos if you were mixing around with different boys and that.'

Molly nodded, too depressed to argue. She had been looking forward all week to the disco, ever since Bridget had promised to take her. They sat in silence when the bus finally came, pretending they had not noticed the smartly-dressed woman pulling her child away from them as they boarded, as if they had some sickness that was catching.

The corner shop was still open when they passed it, and Molly grabbed Bridget's arm.

'Let's get something to eat while we watch the telly,' she said. 'We've the money we couldn't use for the disco.'

The girl behind the counter was chatting to a couple of lads from the estate as she gave them their change.

'It's right there in the paper,' she was saying, as the fair-haired boy Bridget had often noticed on the street unfolded the copy of the evening paper on the shelf in front of him. His companion looked over his shoulder as he found the article and whistled.

'That's the blondy one we saw in the gangster pic-ture in the Savoy,' he said. 'I wouldn't put her out with the cat on a cold night!'

'And her husband along with her,' said the girl behind the counter. 'I used to stay in every Saturday night when he was on the telly. Every time he gave that sort of broody look my knees used turn to jelly!'

Then she noticed Bridget and Molly, standing just inside the doorway, and broke off abruptly.

'What do youse want?' she asked sharply.

'Two kit-kats, two cokes and a packet of crisps,' Bridget said, conscious of the stares of the two lads.

'Have you the price of them?' the girl asked suspi-ciously.

Flushing, Bridget slammed a five pound note down on the counter. The girl whipped it up, rang up the price on the cash register and put the change and the plastic bag of goodies down on the counter together, avoiding Bridget's outstretched hand.

'I never trust them ones,' Bridget heard her saying to the lads as they left the shop. 'You'd want eyes in the back of your head when they're around.'

Though she'd often had to listen to such remarks, still Bridget burned with rage as they walked on to the halting site. But when they reached home there was news that made both of them forget all the insults.

'There was a man going around all the caravans,' their mother told them, 'and he said he was making a picture. And he asked loads of ould questions.'

'What sort of questions?' Molly asked.

'About us burning everything when anyone dies, and the cant and that. And would we mind if our caravan was in the picture. Only your Daddy was gone to the pub with the other men, so he said he'd be back tomorrow.'

'Why would one of the settled people want to know about the way travellers talk?' Molly asked in amazement.

'Because the picture's about travellers,' her mother told her. 'And he's looking for three or four families to be in it with the caravans.'

'In the picture?' asked Molly excitedly.

'D'you mean acting and that?' Bridget gasped.

'That kind of thing,' her mother agreed, 'only he said there won't be any talking or anything like that.'

Their ruined evening forgotten, the two girls ran around the various caravans and trailers, which mostly belonged to uncles and cousins and grandparents. Every one of them had had a visit from the strange man, but they too had asked him to come back when the men would be at home, and they too were astonished that anyone who was not a traveller would be interested in their traditions, customs and secret language.

Next morning there was more than the usual number

of men doing odd jobs around the site instead of going off collecting scrap metal or selling car parts, for everyone knew there was a fortune to be made out of films.

'They give you a mint of money,' Bridget and Molly's elder brother Paddy said. 'Even if it's only a corner of an ould trailer they want in their picture!'

So when the man in the showerproof jacket appeared on the site he was quickly surrounded by travellers of all ages.

'Hey, Mister! Can I be in your picture, Mister?' the smaller kids all cried, pushing and jostling and fighting to get his attention, so that it was difficult for him even to make himself heard.

Bridget and Molly hung back shyly on the fringes of the crowd, but after a while the man managed to insist that he would only talk to people in their own caravans or trailers.

'He's starting beyond by the gate,' Paddy said angrily, 'and Martin and Mikey will get all the money that's going.'

'Didn't he say he wanted our caravan?' his father reminded him.

In the end, after a great deal of hard bargaining, it seemed that everyone would get something out of it, though not the fortunes that Paddy had predicted. Only two caravans and a trailer were wanted in close up, but the film people were willing to give smaller sums for using all the kids in one particular sequence and a few longshots of the whole site. The man also picked a few families as extras and, to Bridget and Molly's delight, theirs was one of the lucky families.

When word got out around Coolock that the film unit

would be coming, a buzz of excitement could be heard around the whole district. The next time Bridget and Molly went into the corner shop, the girl behind the counter looked at them with curiosity rather than the usual suspicion. As they were leaving, Bridget heard her saying to the customer who was buying her weekly copy of *Woman's Own*:

'And to think they're going to be making some of the picture on that halting site! I can tell you, I'll be minding the shop from outside the door that week, hail, rain or snow, in case I'd get a gawk at your man!'

'D'you think will we get to chat with him?' Molly asked Bridget breathlessly.

'Who?' asked her father suspiciously, looking up from the record player he'd salvaged from the dump and was trying to fix.

'The fella we saw on the telly that time,' Bridget explained. 'The black-haired lad that's in the picture.'

'Have nothing to do with blackguards the like of that,' her father ordered promptly.

'His wife is with him in the picture,' Bridget told him, but her father was not impressed.

'Putting away one woman and marrying another's no bother to the blackguards on the pictures,' he said. 'Stay away from him, you, even if he's married itself.'

'You won't get to meet him,' her mother pointed out. 'Film stars are all big snobs. Worse even than the real settled people.'

'You won't even see him,' Paddy said knowingly, 'if he's not in the same bit of the picture. He'll stay inside in his trailer.'

'Does he live in a trailer too?' Molly asked in wonder, but Paddy laughed.

'Only when he'd be making a picture,' he told her. 'Other times he'd be in a house bigger than Beaumont Hospital, so he'll hardly be chatting to traveller girls.'

'I'd be half afraid to be next or near him if he was standing there in the door this minute,' Bridget said, disappointed.

But when the day came and the procession of cars and trucks and trailers arrived, Bridget quickly spotted the familiar figure, standing talking to the man in the showerproof jacket. To her surprise, he was dressed just like her father.

'I thought he'd be all on for the style,' she said to Molly.

'You're a real eejit,' Paddy told her. 'Isn't he meant to be a traveller in the picture?'

Just then the man in the showerproof jacket came over and told them what he wanted them to do. Bridget had only to stand in the doorway of their caravan, looking across to where the children were playing, while the black-haired man, dressed like her father, walked towards her. Then his wife, who was not meant to be his wife in the picture, called after him and he turned back and said something to her.

It all seemed very simple to Bridget and she was surprised at the fuss made over it. There was a whole crowd of men in their corner of the site; not just what she knew must be a cameraman, and the man holding out a long pole, or the ones angling big lamps, but all sorts of people who seemed to be doing nothing but standing around watching. In the midst of them was a young woman at a small table with a typewriter and a notebook and a little camera of her own, while more women kept darting out and dabbing at the faces of the two stars and messing with their hair.

Even when one of the men shouted 'Action!' and the black-haired man started to walk towards her, the man in the showerproof jacket said something and everyone stopped and went back to the beginning again. This happened several times and, even when they were not stopped and got to the point where the man talked to his wife, they still did it all over again.

'You must think we're all mad!' said a pleasant voice at her side and she saw it was the black-haired man himself, that her mother had said would be far too snobby to talk to her.

'Why do you keep doing it over?' she asked him.

'Because each time some little thing goes wrong.'

'It all looked the very same to me,' Bridget said.

'Well now, the last time the sun suddenly came out and cast a big shadow, so the picture wouldn't match up with the one just before it,' he explained, 'and the time before that, the little lad that jumps over the barrel ran out a bit too far and got in the way of the camera.'

Bridget shook her head in puzzlement.

'It's a crazy way to make a living right enough,' he grinned, and Bridget flushed to think he had read her thoughts so easily. 'But when you see it all put together I hope you'll think it was worth it.'

'Will the picture be shown in town when it's finished?'

'Of course,' he said. 'Better than that, the director's promised to have a special showing for everyone that's in it.'

'Even the travellers?' Bridget asked in amazement.

'Of course,' he said. 'We couldn't do it without you, could we?'

'He's not a bit snobby,' she told Molly that evening. 'He was just ordinary, but real decent. And asking all the time about the way travellers do things.'

'I know,' Molly chimed in. 'When his wife was tying up the pony, she kept saying to me: *Am I doing it right?*'

A few evenings later, Molly and Bridget went into the corner shop for the messages and at once the girl behind the counter stopped serving.

'Did you see your picture in the paper?' she called out to them. 'You lucky things! I wish I was you!'

Stunned, Bridget and Molly looked at the newspaper she was holding out to them. Their own laughing faces looked back at them as they stood in front of their caravan beside the black-haired man, laughing at something he had said to them.

'I never knew they were after taking a snap of us that time' Bridget cried. 'I'd have put a comb in my hair. It's terrible wild.'

'I think you look great,' the girl behind the counter said enviously. 'And talking to your man and all. What's he like?'

'A bit like my cousin Martin,' Bridget told her, 'only he'd be more easily swindled like, being only one of the settled people, d'you know?'

'What about the blondy one he's married to?' asked the fair-haired lad the shopgirl had been serving. 'Did you meet her too?'

'Of course,' Molly said. 'Didn't she take a sup of tea

with us in the caravan yesterday?'

'What's *she* like?' the fair-haired boy's companion asked eagerly.

'Grand,' Molly told him, 'only a bit clumsy, like, with a pony.'

'Will you tell us all about the filming?' the girl behind the counter asked.

'Another time,' Bridget told her. 'If we don't hurry now me daddy'll murder me. He's waiting on the sup of milk for his tea.'

'When you've the time,' the girl begged, 'maybe you'd come up to the house and tell me mammy about it. She can't get out much now with the arthritis, and she's only dying to hear about it.'

'Maybe tomorrow,' Bridget nodded, picking up the messages.

'I wish our bit of the picture wasn't finished,' Molly said, as they walked back to the site. But Bridget laughed.

'The telling of it won't be finished for many a long day,' she said.

Maeve Friel *is one of Ireland's most distinguished writers for young people. Her novel* The Deerstone *was shortlisted for the Bisto Book of the Year Award in 1992,* Distant Voices *was shortlisted for both the Bisto and RAI awards in 1995, and* The Lantern Moon *won a Bisto Merit Award and was shortlisted for the RAI award in 1997. Her next book,* The Lions of Benismael, *is due in 1999.*

THE SPANISH DONKEY

by Maeve Friel

When Ignacio Vilanueva, better known as Nacho, came to Dublin to learn English, he lived with the Hunts. And because he hit it off so well with Neil Hunt, better known as Hunty, Hunty went back with him to Spain for the summer holidays.

Nacho's father Antonio ('Call me Toncho') picked them up at the airport. As they came out of the terminal into the blinding white afternoon sun, a noisy coach-load of tourists, all as red as lobsters and dressed in flowery Bermuda shorts, pushed through the revolving doors. One of them was carrying an enormous stuffed donkey with a silly straw hat.

'Tourists!' thought Hunty, tossing his head. 'I wouldn't be seen dead with a Spanish donkey!'

They drove along the coast past apartment blocks that looked like walls of white Lego bricks and then up into the mountains, speeding past lemon groves and sleepy sun-bleached villages until, at last, Toncho rounded a corner and screeched to an emergency stop behind a three-wheeled bread van.

Ahead of them an apparently endless line of cars stretched up the hill. Some of the drivers had got out and were standing about waving their arms and shouting at the tops of their voices.

'What's going on?' Nacho shouted to the bread-man.

'It's a demonstration. Some madman has blocked the bridge up to San Bernardo with a tractor and won't budge.'

'I knew it,' groaned Toncho. 'I bet it's your grandfather, doing his animal rights thing.'

'Come on,' said Nacho, grabbing Hunty by the sleeve and pulling him out of the car. Hunty scrambled after him as Nacho raced towards the stone bridge where an old man in a jaunty-looking panama hat was parading in front of the tractor with a large home-made placard. Nacho threw himself around the old man's neck.

'So you're the boy from Ireland?' the grandfather said when Nacho finally let him go. 'I'm Ramon, but most people call me Moncho.'

'What does your placard say?' asked Hunty.

'*No to the Barbaric Antics of the San Bernardinos*,' Nacho translated. 'They're shooting pigeons up there today.'

Hunty put on a mock-pained expression. He had once taken a potshot at a pigeon on a roof with an air rifle.

'It's part of the summer festival in San Bernardo,' the old man explained. 'They hold a pigeon shoot every year. Not clay pigeons, you understand. Real ones, thousands of them.'

As he spoke, a long volley of rifle shots echoed around the valley. Then another, and another.

'It's a massacre,' said Moncho. 'The whole fiesta from start to finish is barbarous.'

Behind them the angry drivers honked their horns. 'Enough is enough, old man,' shouted one of them.

'You've made your protest. Now let all of us get on with our own business.'

'Yes, come on,' agreed Nacho's father. 'Pigeons are pests anyway.'

The grandfather's home was pretty as a picture post-card. It was an old stone farmhouse with green shutters on the windows and a red tiled roof. Scarlet geraniums spilled out of terracotta urns on the balconies. As Hunty got out of the car, a lizard scuttled across his path. Another one was clamped to the front door like a bizarre door-knocker.

Inside everything was cool and white. The grandfa-ther led the boys into his study and threw open the shut-ters. Sunlight flooded in. Hunty saw shelves of strange brass instruments, a stuffed owl and enormous fossils — ammonites and stony broad-winged fish and coiled snails as large as a man's fist. On the desk was a trans-parent snakeskin a metre long. Its prominent eyesock-ets still bulged where the snake had wriggled out of its outgrown scaly coat. Hunty jumped back.

'Isn't it wonderful?' said Moncho. 'I found it in the orange groves the other day.'

Nacho grinned. 'Grandfather is always finding things like that. He's animal-crazy.'

Up on the top shelf, the stuffed owl winked down at Hunty.

'That's Chelo, his pet,' said Nacho.

Snakes? Lizards? A snail fossil as big as a grape-fruit? A pet owl? Yes, thought Hunty, this grandfather was cool.

Later on, as darkness fell, they were hanging over the balcony watching a string of goats coming down the hillside. The night was perfectly still except for the tinkling of the goats' bells. Suddenly there was an almighty explosion. An enormous cascade of gold and scarlet streamers arced across the sky and fell back into the valley in a shower of shooting stars.

'Fireworks!' yelled Nacho. 'Can we go up to San Bernardo? Please?'

'Don't even think about it,' said Moncho. 'None of us is setting a foot in the village until the fiesta is over.'

'But why?' asked Hunty.

'Because of the wretched donkey,' said Moncho.

Hunty raised his eyebrows, prepared for anything.

Every year, Nacho explained, the villagers of San Bernardo crowned a donkey during the fiesta and put it up on the roof of the belltower. 'It's a sort of mascot.'

Grandfather Moncho snorted. 'Mascot, my eye,' he said. 'That poor beast will be turned loose and ridden to exhaustion on the last day of the festival. Every class of idiot will be racing it round and round the streets. Young, old, rich or ugly, they all have a go on it. And the merrier they get, the more they drive the unfortunate creature on. I've been trying to have it banned for years.'

As he spoke another ear-splitting firework exploded, casting a rainbow of colour across the sky and lighting up the belltower on the hill where the donkey was tethered on the roof.

'Poor beast,' Moncho said. 'If I was a younger man...Direct Action, that's the only way to put a stop to it.'

'Don't be silly, father,' Carmen, Nacho's mother, cut him off. 'It's harmless entertainment. Anyway, the only casualties are the people who get kicked by the ass or thrown off its back. Now, it's bedtime for you boys.'

'Can we sleep on the balcony?' asked Nacho.

His mother shrugged. 'If you don't mind the mosquitoes...'

'What's wrong with mosquitoes?' asked the grandfather. 'Don't they have to eat too?'

The boys lay on their tummies on two sunbeds, watching the sky until the very last firework had faded. As the lights went out in the village and the last trickle of revellers staggered homewards, a donkey began to bray, bellowing so loudly it woke every dog in the valley and set off a chain of angry barking.

'Poor donkey,' said Hunty. 'It must be terrified up there alone.'

'Or else it just didn't want the firework display to stop,' said Nacho, grinning.

'When is this donkey-racing?' asked Hunty, scratching a bite on his leg.

'After the procession tomorrow. Well, that's today, really.'

They looked up at the tower and then at one another, a mad gleam in their eyes. Direct Action.

Dawn had just broken when the boys tiptoed out through the sleeping house. Unseen, behind the shuttered window, Moncho saw them leave. They climbed the hill to San Bernardo, stepping over burnt-out rockets and drifts of confetti. In the main square, they slipped behind a statue in the church porch beside the belltower. The donkey, out of sight in its lofty prison on the tower roof, dreamed on.

At five minutes to six, a stocky dishevelled figure

lurched out of the alleyway opposite the tower, pulling his braces up over a very large belly.

'Toto,' whispered Nacho, 'the bellringer.'

Toto paused at the door of the belltower to relight a crooked cheroot. The boys could hear his heavy iron keyring jangling as he turned the key in the lock. A few minutes later, peeking out from the porch, they saw him lean over the roof, toss his cigar butt over the edge and turn back to unfasten the bellrope. At the fourth peal, the donkey threw back its head and brayed and bellowed in protest. Down in the orchards, a cock began to crow. Nacho counted out six bells. There was a short pause, then the bells started to ring out a second time.

'Why's he doing that?' whispered Hunty.

'It's traditional here. He always rings them twice.'

'We'll never get away with this,' said Hunty, imagining that soon every baby in the whole of San Bernardo would start yelling for breakfast and every dog begin to howl.

'Relax. Nobody gets up early during the fiestas: they've only just gone to bed. Now let's go.'

They ran out of hiding and snatched the iron key that Toto had left in the lock.

A few minutes later, the bellringer came lumbering down from the roof, humming tunelessly. The boys peered out from behind the statue. Toto pulled the door closed behind him, then swore as he saw the empty lock. He stepped back into the square and looked back up at the tower, scratching his stubbly chin. 'I must have taken the darned thing up with me,' he muttered. 'Well, it's safe enough there until seven o'clock.' And he ambled off towards the alley, puffing away at another stinking cheroot.

Nacho and Hunty pushed open the heavy wooden door and entered the tower, its interior dazzling with a new coat of whitewash. The ancient staircase zigzagged to the open roof in a series of sloping brick ramps. The boys raced each other up and arrived, panting, on the top landing.

The donkey was in the far corner champing on a bale of hay. It slowly raised its head and looked at them with reproachful eyes. More unwelcome visitors, it seemed to be saying.

It was a pretty donkey, sandy-coloured with a thick line of wiry upright hair running halfway down its back, and a low-slung barrel of a tummy. Its ears poked out from a crown of golden paper flowers.

'Poor Dina,' said Nacho, stroking its ears. 'We've come to rescue you.'

'Is that its name — Dina?'

'It's what grandfather and I always call them. After San Bernardo.'

Hunty looked puzzled.

'Bernardino if it's a male, Bernardina if its a female. Dino or Dina for short. Easy.'

'Easy,' agreed Hunty. He was beginning to get the hang of the nickname business. 'Now what do we do?'

'We take her down. Leave the key on the wall for Toto to find.'

Nacho untied the rope which tethered the donkey, all the time tickling her ears and speaking to her in a quiet soothing voice. The donkey looked at him doubtfully from under her long eyelashes. They coaxed her across the small square roof to the start of the first ramp. Dina looked down the slope and refused to budge.

'Come on. Good girl. Walk on.'

Dina's long ears flicked forwards and sideways like little antennae. She took one careful step on to the ramp. And stopped.

'Come on,' said Hunty, tugging gently on the rope, 'we're trying to rescue you.'

Dina hung her head and dug in her heels.

'I don't suppose you've got a carrot,' said Nacho.

'Sure,' replied Hunty. 'I never leave home without one.'

Nacho gave the donkey a little slap on her behind. Dina did not move.

'Go and get a handful of that,' Nacho said, pointing at the hay. 'Hold it towards her but out of her reach.'

Hunty walked slowly down the ramp backwards, holding the hay at arm's length. 'Come on, Dina, good girl. Walk on.'

The donkey stretched out her neck, straining to reach the hay. Hunty took another step backwards. 'Come on, Dina, breakfast.'

Dina daintily raised a hoof and placed it cautiously on the slope. Nacho led her forward, coaxing her down the ramp with a stream of encouraging words. At the first landing, she bellowed angrily, jerked her head back and showed a fierce amount of long dark teeth. She stopped stock still and eyed Nacho and Hunty. It was plain she was going nowhere unless she had that hay. When they let her have a mouthful, she bared her teeth again at them as if she was laughing, and kicked Hunty's shin.

'Ouch, that hurt!' he shouted, hopping from one foot

to the other.

'Come on, Hunty, hurry up. At this rate, Toto will be back before we've got her out.'

'It's not my fault. Stupid donkey. Whose idea was this anyway?'

'It's okay. She's just suspicious.'

'Shall we leave her back?'

'No way. Come on.'

With a lot more pushing and shoving and pulling on the rope, they got her moving again. She even trotted down the next ramp as if it was just one of the steep mountain tracks she was used to. Then they turned the corner on to the landing. The sun was shining through the slit of the window, casting a narrow rectangle of light on the dark brick floor. Dina stopped dead in front of it and hung her head.

'Why has she stopped again?' asked Hunty, exasperated.

'She's afraid of the light. Donkeys will stop dead in front of a hole in the road rather than walk around it, you know. They just don't like anything unfamiliar.'

'If you're such an expert on donkeys, why did you think we could get her out of here?' snapped Hunty. 'The whole village will be up soon.' He limped forward and looked through the narrow window. Dina took one cautious step forward.

'Fantastic, Hunty! You're blocking the light! Stand where you are until I get her past you.'

Things were going better until, halfway down the next ramp, Dina suddenly twisted her head around and sank her teeth into Nacho's arm.

'Hey, we're trying to save your life, stupid!' he cried

out. 'Look at those teeth-marks on my sweatshirt! I'll probably get rabies or something!'

The donkey stared sorrowfully back at him from under her lopsided crown of golden flowers.

'Maybe one of these would help,' said Hunty, rooting around in the pocket of his jeans and pulling out a packet of peppermints.

Dina raised her head and sniffed. Hunty laid a sweet on his palm and held it towards her. She stepped forward. Hunty stepped back. She stretched out her long neck and snatched the sweet.

'Brilliant! Hold out another!' said Nacho, rubbing at his sore arm.

The trio moved forward cautiously, with Dina snapping and jerking at the rope as she strained to reach the peppermint. At each landing, they let her have one, watching her as she chewed it with a triumphant gleam in her eyes. Then they had to start the whole business over again.

As they turned the last corner, Dina's nostrils flared excitedly as she caught the whiff of the outside world. Hunty opened the massive wooden door of the tower and peeped out. The sleepy village slumbered on. Nacho took Dina's paper crown and hung it over the doorknob.

Out in the open, Dina was a different character. She broke into a trot as they led her behind the church and past the tightly-shuttered houses. She only stopped once when a cloud of crickets, like dried-up yellow leaves, startled her by rising up and resettling on the fleshy leaves of a prickly pear tree. The last peppermint got her moving again.

When Toto sheepishly broke the news that the donkey had escaped, the village went crazy. Men stood under the flapping bunting in the square and declared that it was a disgrace, a catastrophe.

But, in the end, a fiesta is a fiesta. There was a procession to hold, a bandstand to set up, more fireworks to organise and a festival queen to be chosen. Everybody was too busy to waste time looking for a badtempered scrawny old ass.

So, while San Bernardo partied on, Dina relaxed in the lemon orchard behind grandfather Moncho's house. She ate a little grass, nibbled a carrot or two, snapped impatiently at Hunty when he was too slow unwrapping the next packet of peppermints, and smacked her tail at Nacho when he tried to top up her water-dish.

Snoozing under his panama hat, the grandfather smiled.

'You could take Dina home with you, Hunty,' he said. 'A Spanish souvenir.'

Hunty limped into the shade of a lemon tree to scratch his swelling mosquito bites. He said nothing. Dina hee-hawed fit to burst.

Marilyn Taylor *is well-known in adult circles as a former school librarian and Committee member of Children's Books Ireland. To thousands of young people, however, she's best known as the author of* Call Yourself a Friend? Could This Be Love I Wondered? *(an International Youth Library White Ravens Selection), and* Could I Love a Stranger? *She is an admirable person, and in real life doesn't ask half as many questions as the titles of her novels might suggest.* A Shipboard Romance, *one of her rare short stories, was written for this collection.*

A SHIPBOARD ROMANCE

by Marilyn Taylor

'I think I'm going to be sick' groaned Suzanne as the ship gave a slow, ominous lurch. 'You shouldn't have got me those chips.' She pushed away the soggy paper plate with its remaining chips congealing in a pool of blood-red ketchup.

Kathy patted her best friend's shoulder sympathetically. 'Miss Kelly said it's better to have something in your stomach —'

'Don't say stomach,' wailed Suzanne, leaning her head tragically against the cool thick glass of the window. Drama was Suzanne's best subject.

Kathy checked out her own stomach as the boat gave another roll. Slightly queasy, but not too bad. At least, not yet.

'You're so lucky you don't get sea-sick,' muttered Suzanne. There was an implication that Kathy's stomach was somehow less sensitive than Suzanne's.

'I'd better see if I can find Miss Kelly,' said Kathy, standing up gingerly. The boat lurched again, and a messy jumble of plates, cups and half-empty Coke cans slid across the table top.

Suzanne gave a shriek and clutched Kathy. 'Don't leave me on my own,' she wailed. 'Suppose the ship sinks and we have to get to the lifeboats? Anyway, Miss Kelly was looking a bit green last time I saw her.'

Yeah, that was true, thought Kathy. And she'd noticed Mr O'Connor disappearing into the Duty Free shop.

At this stage of the school trip to Stratford-on-Avon the students and their teachers had boarded the ferry back to Ireland in the hope, on both sides, that they could have a bit of a rest from each other. Five days of togetherness had tested their collective tolerance almost to the limit.

But where were the others? Kathy gazed round the almost deserted cafeteria.

There were two fellas at the next but one table. One had his head down on the table, buried in his arms. His companion was carefully making his way towards the drinks machine.

As he staggered past their table Kathy saw he was holding what was unmistakably a handful of white paper vomit bags, like the ones in the seat-pockets of planes. The bags appeared to be unused, so far anyway.

Kathy's eyes met his and he gave her a tentative smile. Nice smile, she thought.

'Just getting water for my friend,' he said shyly. Nodding towards Suzanne he added,

'Does your friend wants some?'

Kathy smiled gratefully. She turned to Suzanne, whose soft mass of fair hair had gone lank, her usually glowing skin grey and pallid.

'Suzanne,' Kathy whispered into her ear. 'D'you want a drink of water?' Suzanne nodded without opening her eyes.

The fella set off as the boat heaved again. Suzanne gave another groan. '... sick', was all she managed this time.

Kathy pushed a wad of tissues into Suzanne's inert hand. I've got to keep on top of things, to look after Suzanne, she told herself, trying to ignore the uncomfortable stirrings inside her.

After all, looking after Suzanne was more or less her role in life.

The boy came back and set down a paper cup, the water slopping out on to the table top. 'Sorry,' he said, with an unmistakably English accent. As Kathy reached out to steady the cup their hands touched. She felt another peculiar feeling in her stomach. The seasickness, she thought. Or was it?

'Hey Paul! Where's the bloody water?' The other fella had raised his head and was glaring over at them.

'Coming,' called Paul, and grinning apologetically at Kathy and Suzanne he sped back to his friend.

As Suzanne took tiny sips from the paper cup, mopping her damp forehead with the tissues, Kathy thought back over the last few days. The trip had been fun on the whole. The Royal Shakespeare Company's performance of Hamlet, the class's set text, seemed ages ago now, like a dream. They'd all fallen for the golden-haired, husky voiced Hamlet, gorgeous in black tights, a huge gold medallion round his neck, as he agonised his way through 'To be or not to be,' drawing every last ounce of feeling from the familiar words.

All except Suzanne, that is, who in the interval had tossed her head and said she thought Hamlet was a nerd. Kathy had rather liked Hamlet's friend Horatio, laughing and handsome in a scarlet and silver cloak. But Suzanne had said he was naff.

An announcement crackled over the loudspeaker, its distorted sound hard to make out. Something about a 'swell' and 'fresh to strong' and 'gale warning'. It didn't sound encouraging. Kathy hoped she hadn't missed something vital, like information as to where to go if the alarm sounded.

Peering out at the mixture of rain and spray streaming down the outside of the window, she could dimly make out people standing about on the deck, or moving slowly and deliberately, like figures in a dream.

'Maybe we should go outside,' she ventured. 'The fresh air...'

'Don't say fresh air,' whispered Suzanne. She sank her head down on to the table with a groan. 'Get me something to be sick in,' she commanded.

Kathy looked over at the two fellas. The sea-sick one was throwing up into one of the bags, while Paul looked on anxiously. Kathy caught his eye and he half rose.

'Could we borrow one of those bags?' she called. How stupid, she thought. We're hardly going to give it back, especially if it was used,

Paul hurried over with the vomit bag. She noticed his eyes were a soft brown, and he was wearing an X-Files T-shirt.

'D'you feel okay?' he asked Kathy.

It struck her that of all the fellas who'd been around her and Suzanne, at discos, at parties, on the bus from school, anywhere, Paul was the first one who'd ever taken any interest in her rather than Suzanne. That's probably only because Suzanne's sick, she told herself. But it made a pleasant change to be noticed for once.

'Well, I'm trying not to think about my...' She stopped, just in time.

'Stomach?' he said.

Suzanne jerked up from her recumbent position, looked round wildly, and grabbed a bag from the table. They all waited, but nothing happened.

'Paul, get over here,' shouted his friend from the other table. He'd stopped throwing up and was looking pissed off. 'I need a Coke.'

Paul leaped up obediently. 'Would you like one?' he asked Kathy. She shook her head, hoping he would come back.

When he did come back Suzanne had her eyes closed again. He sat down opposite them, looking at Kathy. 'Um, what's your name?'

'I'm Kathy. And this is Suzanne. We're on our way back to Dublin from a school trip.'

'I'm Paul,' he said. Indicating his companion he went on, 'Adam won a weekend for two in Dublin in a school raffle.' He paused. 'It's not a very good start.'

There was a silence. Just my luck to meet someone nice and have people being sick all round us, thought Kathy .

'It's supposed to be a help if you can look at the sea,' he said hesitantly. 'At least I think so.'

'Yeah, I heard that,' agreed Kathy. She lowered her voice. 'But I don't know how I can get Suzanne out there.'

Suzanne opened her eyes. Seeing Paul she put her hand to her head in tragic mode, rather like Hamlet had. 'I'm dying,' she intoned.

'What about some fresh air?' said Paul cheerily.

'You're sure to feel better on deck.'

To Kathy's surprise Suzanne managed a wan smile. 'If you think so,' she whispered, fluttering her eye-lashes at Paul.

Paul seemed unmoved. He turned to Kathy. 'We could bring her out first,' he suggested, as though Suzanne was a parcel, 'and then we could come back for Adam.'

They looked over at Adam, who was sitting like a zombie staring straight ahead, clutching his paper cup.

'Okay,' agreed Kathy. 'Better make it quick.'

'Yeah,' agreed Paul. 'While he's in a trance.'

Kathy and Paul hoisted Suzanne to her feet. Her knees buckled, but she fell against Paul rather than Kathy. They both gripped her arms and gently manoeu-vred her across the cafeteria, grabbing at anything to hand as they picked their way among the recumbent figures in sleeping bags. The floor tilted beneath their feet.

Outside on the deck the wind, with a fresh salty tang, roared round them. They struggled over to the rail, lined with white-faced passengers, some throwing up, others staring mesmerised at the huge expanse of grey water and white-crested waves crashing angrily against the side of the ship.

Kathy thought she noticed Miss Kelly leaning over the side, but Suzanne was clasping her so tightly she couldn't move to look more closely.

'Stay with me, Kathy,' whimpered Suzanne. 'I might need you.'

'I'm just going with Paul to get his friend,' said Kathy, unclasping Suzanne's arms with difficulty and hooking them over the rail to hold her upright. 'You'll be fine.'

'No, no, I might be blown overboard,' moaned Suzanne. 'Where are the life boats?'

'She's a bit over the top, isn't she,' Paul muttered to Kathy. 'It's not that bad.'

'She always makes a drama about things,' whispered Kathy.

'So does Adam,' said Paul.

The ship lurched and a heavy shower of spray sluiced over them. Suzanne screamed.

Paul and Kathy looked at each other. 'We look like drowned rats,' he said. And he reached out and brushed dribbles of water from Kathy's face. 'Come on,' he said. 'We'd better go back for Adam.'

Leaving a furious Suzanne clinging to the rail, squeezing water from her drenched hair, they started back.

The boat gave another heave and Kathy staggered. Paul put his arm round her and for a moment his dripping face was close to hers. It felt great. Suzanne would be furious.

But it was worth it.

Back in the cafeteria Adam was standing up unsteadily. Despite his lank ponytail and pale sweaty face Kathy guessed that when he wasn't sea-sick he might be gorgeous, the sort of fella everyone wanted for a boyfriend.

He said coldly to Paul, 'Where've you been?' His angry blue eyes swung round to Kathy. 'Who's this?' he asked disdainfully, as though she was some bit of rubbish Paul had picked up.

'Kathy,' she said.

Paul asked him hastily, 'Feeling any better?' As he spoke the ship swayed and shook. They heard a distant sound of smashing crockery.

'I feel like shit,' grunted Adam.

Paul glanced apologetically at Kathy.

None of us can help our friends, she thought. But maybe we can help ourselves. Why were she and Paul acting like nannies? She'd always run around after Suzanne, taken whatever she'd dished out, always been terrified Suzanne would abandon her, and then she'd have no friends. But maybe the truth was the opposite - she was so tied in with Suzanne that no-one else came near her.

Until Paul.

'You'll feel better out on deck,' Paul said to Adam, rather more firmly than he'd spoken before. To her surprise Adam shrugged and stood up. Paul and Kathy gripped one arm each and led him out on deck.

Suzanne was standing by the rail in the exact position they'd left her, a bedraggled figure staring out to sea. She turned to Kathy with a scowl, which was miraculously replaced with a long-suffering smile when she saw Adam.

Paul and Kathy hooked Adam to the rail beside Suzanne. He began to say something to Paul in a complaining tone, when Suzanne whispered in his ear in her huskiest voice.

'D'you feel like I feel?'

Adam took a look at her and nodded. The two of them exchanged a long glance.

Kathy, watching them, could have sworn that natural colour began to return to both their faces at the same moment. Adam straightened up and combed his pony-tail with his fingers. Suzanne, without taking her eyes off Adam, started rooting in her bag, for what Kathy guessed was her dark purple lipstick. Adam casually pushed up the sleeve of his denim jacket to display an elaborate tattoo. Their eyes were still locked together.

Kathy felt a gentle touch. It was Paul's hand on her shoulder. He gave her a little conspiratorial smile and jerked his head towards the other side of the deck, where there was an empty space beside the lifeboats.

'Coming?' he asked. Kathy felt a warm glow flowing through her. She stopped to check. It definitely wasn't the sea-sickness.

Further down the deck she spotted Mr O'Connor supporting a white-faced Miss Kelly into the lounge. Behind them were several of their school group in dripping anoraks. They stared as Kathy gave them a cheery wave.

Then, arms linked, and without a backward glance, Kathy and Paul tiptoed away.

Frank Murphy *is a former national teacher whose writing manages to be - at the same time - both up-to-date and timeless. His first novel for young people,* Lockie and Dadge, *won both the Eilis Dillon Memorial Award and a Merit Award in the Bisto Book of the Year Awards in 1996. He is a gentleman.* The Killing Fields of Moyle *is an unpublished story.*

THE KILLING FIELDS OF MOYLE

by Frank Murphy

'Timmy, will you come hunting?' Billy Walker asked.

'Yeah, yeah! I will.' Timmy Cooney was excited. 'Who is going?'

'Johnny Dunne. He told me to get another one.'

'What about dogs?' Timmy asked. He knew there had to be dogs.

'We have dogs, but Johnny said to bring sticks.'

The men of Moyle had been hunters for as long as the town was there, and even before that, from the time that stone-age tribes first set up their wattle huts by the Awbeg river.

Timmy had often watched hunters marching home after a day in the fields outside the town, old clothes mud-spattered, tired dogs, with heads low and tongues out, panting, dead rabbits, held by the hind legs, like fur rags studded with glassy eyes. The men came with a proud walk and the look of conquerors. Timmy would love to be one of those hunters, and to walk proudly past the envious eyes of the other young ones.

Now his chance had come. This was the real thing. This wasn't like pointing a hurley and shouting 'Bang!' and the 'enemy' dropping dead. That nonsense was over. Oh, yes! This was man's stuff. He would need his

47

heavy boots for this work.

He ran home and clumped up the stairs, two steps at a time. His mother heard him rummaging in his wardrobe.

'What are you up to, Timmy?' she called.

'We're going out the road for a walk,' he said, which, if it wasn't the full truth, wasn't exactly a lie either.

He took his father's walking-stick from the hall-stand and hared down the street to meet the others near the railway station. There were four in all, because Benny Healy, who was a bit older than the other three, had joined them. He had been out with the men on a few Sundays, so he knew what it was about. They had two dogs, Dunne's brindled mongrel, half greyhound, half Labrador, and Walker's wheaten terrier.

'Come on,' said Johnny Dunne grandly. 'Today we hunt, tomorrow we dine on rabbit stew!'

Timmy was delighted. With Benny along it was really serious. Benny was a bit old for games, an old man in a boy's shape. He never smiled, as if the world were too serious a place for levity.

They walked along, and Timmy's mind was making pictures of dogs barking and he and the others shouting in a wild chase after rabbits and hares across wide fields.

Denis Kennedy was sitting on the garden wall of his house.

'Where are you all going?' he asked.

'Where do you think?' Billy said. 'Can't you see we're going hunting?'

'Can I come too?'

'No!' Johnny Dunne said firmly. 'You're too young.'

'No, I'm not. I can race Billy Walker.'

'It's rough country out there,' Johnny told him. 'You couldn't keep up.'

'Timmy, can I go with you?' the little fellow pleaded. 'I'll give you my bike for a whole day.'

'No, Denis. I'm sorry,' Timmy said.

'How is it I can go with you every other day?'

'You can't come!' Benny Healy said quietly, and there was something final about the way he said it.

Soon they had left the town behind and were headed out the Shanadoon Road.

'Where are we going?' Timmy asked.

'To Meehan's Fort,' Johnny Dunne said. 'It's alive with rabbits. They come out and almost ask to be caught.'

Traffic was light, and they walked along the centre of the road. Johnny walked ahead, whacking the side of his leg with an ash-plant and calling the dogs to heel when they strayed.

'When we get there, Timmy, I'll show you what to do' he said.

The February air was cold, though the sun shone from a hard blue sky. After days of heavy rain the countryside was washed clean.

Benny climbed over a stone wall near a bridge on the Awduv River. The others followed and they walked through the fields on the river bank. The Awduv was in flood, a rush of brown water sweeping along below the tops of the banks.

Timmy shouted in mock terror as Billy caught him and pretended to throw him into the water. They frolicked about, squelching through the wet fields, chasing each other in high spirits. The dogs bounded around them, barking furiously.

'Stop it! Stop it!' Benny Healy said, so savagely that they stopped at once and looked at his serious face.

'All that racket will frighten them,' he explained.

So they walked silently from field to field, passing through gates, over stiles, or through gaps in the fences.

Timmy lagged a little behind the others as they beat the hedge along the side of a big field. It was a drier field than many of the others, probably because the water ran quickly down its gentle slope. The grass was short and tufted.

'Hul-a-hul! Hul-a-hul!' Benny Healy shouted, so loud and suddenly that Timmy was startled. He looked up and saw the dogs in full gallop after a rabbit that scuttled straight across the field. It was about a hundred metres in front of the dogs, but they were gaining rapidly on it. The boys ran after them as fast as they could, but they were quickly outdistanced by dogs and rabbit.

Timmy stood and watched. He couldn't take his eyes off the rabbit, a ball of brown fur hurtling across the field, its bobbing white scut flashing in terror. He almost felt its fright, and his heart was beating madly.

Soon dogs and rabbit had reached the fence at the opposite side of the field. It was a very wide field, and the boys couldn't see the rabbit at the distance. They could only guess at where it was from the movement of the dogs. They were twisting and turning, wheeling and swerving. They changed direction so often that they must have been dizzy.

Then both dogs collided and fell, turning over and over on the ground. When they stood up again, they had lost sight of the rabbit. They ran about aimlessly for a while. Then Johnny Dunne whistled, and they looked in his direction. They came towards him at speed, heads stretched out, bodies low, skimming the grass as they reached forward with their forepaws on every stride.

Then Timmy saw the rabbit again. It was fleeing ahead of the dogs and coming back across the field towards the boys. They raised their sticks and shouted, trying to turn it back into the path of the dogs, but it dodged between them and then passed Timmy.

The dogs were quite close by then, so close that Timmy could see the wild killing lust in their eyes. He yelled and raised his stick and turned and chased after them. He was well ahead of his companions.

The rabbit was finally cornered at a stonewall fence. As Timmy arrived, the dogs were about to pounce on the little creature, cowering and quivering in fear. It seemed to have given up the battle to stay alive, and just waited for the end.

Timmy screamed and hurled the stick with all his power. It struck Jeff, the mongrel, on the shoulder and spun between his forelegs. Jeff stumbled and fell, and Ronnie, the terrier, tumbled over him. In the confusion that followed, the rabbit scurried into a sprawl of furze about thirty metres away. The dogs chased around, sniffing gingerly at the prickly bushes and barking loudly, but the rabbit did not come out. The boys beat furiously at the bushes, but it was a futile effort.

'It's useless,' Benny Healy said. 'He'll never come out of there.'

Then he turned on Timmy. 'Why did you hit the

dog?' he asked angrily.

'No-no-no!' Timmy said. 'I just threw the stick. It could have hit the rabbit too.'

'The rabbit was a goner if you hadn't thrown the stick. There was no need for you to throw it,' Benny said, and he was furious.

'How was I to know that?' Timmy said.

'Yeah,' Billy said. 'He was throwing at the rabbit.'

'He was,' Johnny agreed.

Benny Healy didn't comment, just walked on with his head down. Timmy's heart was still thumping as he followed the others. They went into Meehan's land and got their first look at the fort, a big grove of trees surrounded by a grassy bank.

They moved out of the sunlight and into the grove. On the ground between the tree trunks there were clumps of briar and withered bracken interlaced with long grass faded to a straw colour.

'Now,' Benny Healy said. 'Do it right this time. You there, Timmy, and you just beyond there, Johnny. Billy, come with me.'

'What'll I do?' Timmy asked.

'If there's a rabbit in there, we want him out of it and running up this way. We'll be up there with the dogs,' Benny said.

'How will I get him out of it?' Timmy asked.

'Just beat the briars with your stick.'

'Do you think there's a rabbit there?' Timmy asked anxiously.

'You won't know that until you've beaten every inch of it. If you do get one to run, shout *Hul-a-hul* so we'll know he's out.'

Of course Benny had done it lots of times, and Johnny Dunne had been out with the men a few times too. It was old hat to them, but for Timmy and Billy it was new and scary. Timmy was still recovering from the previous chase.

When the others had gone and taken up position, he tiptoed nervously round the thicket, trying to see through briar and grass to its hidden centre. The others were out of sight, but he could see Johnny Dunne, fair head bent, beating at another clump about fifty metres further on.

There was no sound within the fort but the swish of Johnny's stick. Timmy crouched behind the thicket, where the others could not see him. He poked timorously at the briars, parting strands of grass and bracken. He discovered that the thick growth of grass, fern, and faded weed was confined to the edge. The centre was bare but for the bramble stems springing out of the ground.

It was not bright enough for him to see clearly what was in there. He shivered as he imagined the furtive movements of small furry bodies with eyes dark as sloes.

At that moment he pushed aside another briar and nearly fell with shock. He had come face to face with a live, breathing rabbit. It was lying at the heart of the thicket, its snout quivering as it sniffed the air for danger. Timmy stared at it, and a look passed between them. He didn't know which of them was more frightened. Then the rabbit panicked and bolted out of the covert on the opposite side.

Timmy stood and stared at its bobbing white scut as

it went on its hoppity run towards Johnny Dunne.

'Hul-a-hul!' Timmy called half-heartedly.

Johnny Dunne looked up and saw the rabbit running towards him. He raised his stick and Timmy uttered a weak cry of horror as he expected the stick to come crashing down on the timid creature. It ran straight at Johnny. There was no escape this time. But Johnny didn't bring down the stick. He held it aloft for a second too long, and when he finally did bring it down, the rabbit had passed under his legs and was gone.

Johnny and Timmy looked at each other for a minute, neither one saying anything, just searching the other's face for signs of guilt, guilt at having let the tribe down. Timmy broke the silence.

'Tough luck, Johnny, you just missed him.' Johnny turned and gave chase, shouting, 'Hul-a-hul. Hul-a-hul!'

Timmy followed at a leisurely trot. Up ahead there was much shouting and dog-barking. Timmy grimaced as he imagined snapping white teeth and tufts of rabbit fur and red blood. When he arrived on the scene, the others were standing there.

'Did ye get him?' he asked.

'Naw. He got away,' Johnny Dunne said.

'Did the dogs hunt him?'

'No,' Billy Walker said. 'Jeff was chasing crows around the field. Ronnie saw him all right, but he wasn't interested.'

Benny Healy was scowling. 'You could have got him, Dunne,' he said. 'He came right by you, and you saw him in plenty of time.'

'That's not true,' Johnny said. 'He came and went so

suddenly I hadn't the time.'

Afterwards they beat along the hedgerows, but without success, and, as the sun went down and twilight began to close in, they made their way to the road and turned for home.

On the way home they joked and laughed about their failure to bag a rabbit.

'Imagine!' said Johnny. 'Ran through my legs and got away.'

'And almost brushed my boot and I didn't see him,' Billy Walker said, and they all laughed. All, that is, except Benny Healy, who kept a sullen silence. When they came to the edge of town, he left them without a word and took another road.

'And Timmy missed the rabbit and hit the dog instead,' Billy said, and they all laughed again, loud and long.

'Never mind,' said Johnny Dunne. 'We'll go again and we'll have better luck.'

Denis Kennedy was leaning on his gate as they came by, their boots muddy, the dogs tired, heads low, tongues out, panting.

'Well, where are all the rabbits?' Denis asked.

They didn't answer.

'Did you catch anything?' Denis persisted.

'Almost,' Johnny Dunne said. 'Almost.'

They swung their sticks and moved on, swaying from side to side in a desperate effort to swagger as they walked into town.

Aislinn O'Loughlin had her first book published when she was fifteen, she's had a book chosen for the International Youth Library's White Ravens series, and her fifth book appeared before her eighteenth birthday. She's too old to be a prodigy any more, but too young to be a doyenne — tough, huh? Meanwhile the film whose script she co-wrote - How To Cheat in the Leaving Cert *- had the honour of being denounced (unseen) in 1998 by an actual politician, so on top of everything else she has pretty good street cred.* Some Sensitive Verse *is a set of poems offering typically thoughtful meditations on wildlife, education and family relationships.*

John Leonard is more used to collaborating with Aislinn's father, Larry. Their Irish Legends series finally takes the retelling of ancient Irish tales into the twentieth century - if not beyond - and one of the series, The Gobán Saor, *was shortlisted for the 1998 Bisto Book of the Year Awards. John's sensitive illustrations here perfectly complement the almost classical restraint of the text.*

SOME SENSITIVE VERSE

by Aislinn O'Loughlin, illustrated by John Leonard

Wally the Wascally Weptile

Wally was a weptile,
A weally wotten one,
He'd wun awound the swamps at night,
Do howwid things for fun

He'd wush between the wushes
Chasing swamp wats wound and wound
Until the wats got ti'ed
And collapsed upon the gwound

Then he'd wam the wabbits
Fwom the meadows to the wivew,
And woll around with laughte'
As the wabbits shooked and shive'ed

Yes, Wally was a weptile,
A weally wotten one,
Until one day at last when he was
Gwounded by his Mum.

His Mum said: 'Wally, weally,
I just can't believe it's twue -
My fwiends awound the swamp
Wepowt such howwid things of you!

My wascally son, I'll gwound you.
You stay inside fowevva!
Wascally weptiles such as you,
They'we weally not that clevva.'

She told him: 'No mo'e wunning,
No mo'e wushing at the wats,
No wamming wabbits into wivveas
'Cos they weally don't like that.'

Now Wally's still a weptile,
And he's still a wotten one,
But he's sowwy 'bout wushing and
                              wamming,
'Cos now he weally can't have any fun

Excuse Me?

My teacher is confusing me,
I wish she'd make up her mind:
Yesterday eighteen was six times three,
Today it's two times nine.

My Dog

My dog has no nose,
Never will, never had.
When I'm asked how he smells
I say: 'Really bad'!!

(Well, I actually say 'awful', but that doesn't rhyme,
does it?)

Sisterly Love

(Or: An Ode to my Little Brother because he's Really
Annoying Me and I Can't Take It Any More and I
Think I'm either Going To Scream or else Kill Him, or
Maybe Both, and I Just Have To Say This because he's
an Annoying Little Twit.)

Shut up, ya little twerp,
Before I Brain Ya!

Aislinn O'Loughlin & John Leonard

Tommy's Teacher Eater

'Excuse me, teacher, please teacher,
Listen to me.'
'Yes?'
'Tommy's got a monster,
Hiding in his desk'

'Oh has he now? Really?
Mmmmhmmm, I see.'
'Please teacher, listen teacher,
You must believe me.

Teacher, it looks really yucky,
All covered in slimy goo.
I want to check if it's still there,
But I can't look - will you?'

'Oh very well, Sam, I'll take a look,
But just so that you'll see...
Good gosh! You're right, there is a
                              monster!
And he's coming after me!'

'Run, teacher!' 'Go, teacher!'
'It's catching up on you!!!...'

'Tommy, now it's eaten another teacher!
'Oh no, what will we do?'...

Michael Scott, as well as being one of Ireland's most popular and internationally successful writers, is probably its most prolific. With almost ninety books in print, translated into a bewildering array of languages, he also has a family and what's called a 'real' job. Some people suspect that he is (at least) twins, but there's definitely only one of him - they broke the mould. I Told You So is a fantasy story set in a universe closer to home than you might think.

I TOLD YOU SO

by Michael Scott

We are the daughters of Palu.

Great is our responsibility as the children of a goddess. At all times we must do her honour, and behave in a way that will bring her honour and make her proud of us.

But this is not always easy.

Palu - all praise to her name - is demanding, and we are sadly fallible. She sets us tasks beyond our poor ability to perform, orders we cannot fulfil no matter how hard we try, and her advice is often incomprehensible.

When we fail, we go to her and offer abject apologies. Sometimes she is forgiving. Sometimes she is capricious and cruel. But whatever her mood, we know that her actions are always for our own good. If we are forgiven, it is because she loves us in spite of our shortcomings. If we are chastised, it is to prevent us from coming to harm in the future. These things she tells us.

All wise is Palu. And very beautiful, with her pale hair and her azure eyes. Throughout my life, just watching her has given me great delight. Would that I could grow into half the beauty she is.

But alas, I cannot. There is only one Palu. But I am honoured to be counted among her daughters.

Behind her exquisitely formed, fine-boned face is a

magnificent mind, quite the most important part of her being. She gladly shares her wisdom, as a goddess should. From earliest childhood, my sisters and I loved to sit at her feet and listen to her teachings.

'Beware the many enemies of our race,' she warned us, long before we had ever seen an enemy, nor yet fully comprehended the term. 'You are my children, and therefore clever. But there are others who are almost as clever, and who would delight in doing you harm.' Her voice, slow and deep and sensual, gave her words added power. 'The Great Dragon, for example, will bind you with evil magic long before you hear his terrible roaring, or smell the stink of his breath. While you stand, paralysed and unmoving, he will crush you like soft fruit and leave you for the carrion eaters. Look not into his lambent eyes, my children.'

When we were very small we shivered with fright at such words. Then great Palu would bend to us and comfort us, spreading the warmth and power of her presence over us like benevolent light until we felt as bold and brave as the goddess herself. With Palu to guide and protect us, we need not tremble at the mention of the Great Dragon. And when we heard them roar and do battle in the night, great Palu would draw us away from the noise and stink of death and foulness and lead us into one of the Secret Places she had prepared with her own blessed limbs. Drawing us close to her, wrapping her soft arms around us, she would lull us asleep with a gentle lullaby and the solid beating of her strong heart.

My sisters Tinka and Tenya were both older than I, though we were all brought forth at the one birthing.

Tenya, Second-Born, in particular was Palu's pride and joy. She had something of our mother's grace and a great deal of her spirit, and many times I caught Palu watching her with an especial fondness. Tinka and I were jealous, though we loved our sister dearly.

But Tenya had a touch of the outlaw about her. She was more and more often in trouble. She ignored every rule, broke every prohibition — and of course she ran into difficulties that only grew worse as she grew older. How many times did I hear great Palu cry out to her, 'You were warned, Tenya! I told you so!' And sometimes, if our mother's anger was great, she would strike out at Tenya, send her tumbling into the dust at her feet.

Tinka and I would look at one another, embarrassed, and then drop our eyes. But Tenya seemed to glory in being contrary. Our home, once a place of sanctuary and learning, rang with the quarrelling voices of great Palu - all glory to her name - and her rebellious second daughter. She seemed set to defy our mother's advice on all things.

Take the matter of Longtooth Demons, for example. Palu had instructed us very thoroughly as to our conduct when confronted by these evil beings. The smaller beasts were cowards, but when they ran in packs they could be deadly, and occasionally attacked our people. There were, however, giants among the demons — beasts who stood nearly as tall as the goddess. Few could stand against them. Palu, however, taught us special prayers to say and magical signs and gestures and ritual movements that would put fear into the foul hearts of the Demons, and make them flee from us.

But Tenya refused to do as she was told. She would

walk right up to a Demon and laugh in his face, mim-
icking him when he bared his fangs, standing tall when
he hissed at her. It was very frightening to see, and
more than once Palu - O Magnificent! - had to inter-
vene at the last moment, to save her favourite child
from irreparable harm. I could never understand why
Tenya would not listen: our mother's advice was for
our own benefit. The Longtooth Demons were said to
delight in the flesh of our people.

For though our mother is a Goddess, we can be hurt
and even slain. And when the Great Dark has overtak-
en us, there will be no Light again. The Once-Secret of
our race, the power to return to the Light thrice three
times, has long been lost to our people. It is said -
though even I do not believe it - that Palu is the last of
her kind, the Many-Living Ones.

My foolish sister was even more careless in the mat-
ter of They Who Smell. Of all the enemies of our peo-
ple - and such marvellous, magical people have many
enemies - They Who Smell were the most disgusting.
Appalling creatures of fur and flabby flesh, everything
about them was an abomination. They were bad-tem-
pered, brutal and brutish. They hunted for sport and
only occasionally for meat. The worst aspect of They
Who Smell, however, was their ignorance. They had no
understanding of elegance or cleanliness, and as for eti-
quette and simple modesty... Well, if I told you some
of the things I personally have seen them do, you would
hardly believe me. I have seen them foul where they
stood and rut in the open, howling out their passion like
base beasts.

One would never expect that a child of Palu would

consort with such beings. Yet Tenya actually sought out their company. The first time it happened it might have been an accident, I suppose. Tinka and I were accompanying our mother on a stroll through the woods when we saw movement in the undergrowth. Palu - bow down at the mention of her name! - froze in her tracks. We followed her example, of course. Then as silently as a shadow she glided forward again, with us right behind her, until we came within sight of a sunlit glade where our Tenya and one of They Who Smell were lolling on the grass together, their flesh actually touching, their heads bent together.

Our mother was shocked beyond description. I thought her eyes would leap from her head. Forgetting her dignity, she shrieked Tenya's name in a voice I had never heard her use before, a voice that turned the marrow in my bones to liquid. The sound sent the beast-creature leaping into the bushes without a backwards glance, leaving Tenya alone in a puddle of sunlight. She did not even have the grace to look embarrassed, but I knew by the look in her eye that she knew she had done wrong.

That night the goddess and Tenya had a terrible fight. Tinka and I hid our heads under our bedclothes, we were so frightened, but their words were clearly audible. 'How could you? To openly consort with such a...such a...' Palu spluttered, at a rare loss for words. 'I fear that there is no crime you might not commit!'

'You exaggerate,' Tenya drawled, and I clearly heard her yawn. Raising my head, I squinted my eyes closed to concentrate the light and peered across the room. Palu and Tenya were standing on either side of the open door. Beyond them the night was silver and black with moonlight.

'Oh, I think not. You have no ideas of the risks you run, my girl. I can protect you as long as you stay with me, but there is a wider world beyond this where nothing can protect you but your own wits - which seem to be sadly lacking.'

Tenya yawned again, making her boredom with lectures obvious. 'You are always warning us about something,' she told Palu, 'but none of the menaces has ever proved as dangerous as you claimed. Many times I have come face to face with the Great Dragon, but he is awkward and cumbersome. I can dance to one side and be gone quicker than his eyes can follow. We are so small I think we are beneath his contempt; certainly I have never seen one pursue any of our people.

'As for the Longtooth Demons, when you first warned us about them you said they were giants. But I have seen none as big as you, or even as big as I am now. What is there to fear in such pigmies?

'And although you have told us that They Who Smell are a murderous clan, that has never been my experience. I think they fear us more than we fear them. I do not fear them, nor do I run from them and give them reason to pursue me, thinking me weak and afraid. I do not threaten them with arcane gestures, nor spit the old words of power at them. I treat them like anyone else and they respond in kind. Could it be, mother, that you are blinded by your own prejudice?'

Hearing these words, Palu lost her temper completely. She lashed out at Tenya with all the strength she possessed, knocking her daughter down, drawing blood high on her cheek. Had it been me, I would have wept and pleaded for mercy, but Tenya just got to her feet again and glared at our mother. 'You will be sorry you ever did that,' she said in a low, deadly tone, wiping the blood away with a deliberately casual movement, then bringing her hand to her mouth to lick at the pink liquid.

The goddess was visibly trembling with rage. 'You are the one who will be sorry, my girl. Continue the way you are going now and you will come to a terrible end. But I will take no further responsibility for one so headstrong and foolish. Just remember, when worse comes to worse and you cry out to me for help... I told you so.'

To my stunned amazement, Tenya promptly turned her back on Palu.

Decency forbids me to repeat what happened then. Suffice it to say that the goddess - long may she reign! - was beside herself with rage. She rained blows down upon Tenya, and for a while I feared she would kill her... and it would be hard to blame her if she did. No-one can insult a goddess with impunity, even her own daughter.

In the end, however, she allowed Tenya to escape with her life. My last glimpse of my sister was of her fleeing into the night, bruised and bloody. But she ran silently, refusing to allow my mother the pleasure of hearing her cry out.

The following morning, Palu simply said that Tenya had gone away for a long time. Afterward she refused to let either Tinka or myself say our sister's name in her, Palu's presence.

But our mother is, in addition to all her other wonderful qualities, a compassionate goddess. At last she relented, and began to speak wistfully of her exiled daughter. 'I fear she may have come to real harm,' said Palu, eyes glistening with tears she was too proud to shed. 'I did my best to teach her, to lead her in the paths of righteousness, but to no avail. Yet even now I cannot abandon her to outer darkness. No.'

She set her chin - O Great Goddess! - and gazed into dimensions lesser beings such as Tinka and myself could not see.

'We shall undertake an odyssey,' Palu announced at last, returning from her reverie. 'A quest in search of she who has gone astray. Wide is the world and very dangerous, but for the sake of my daughter I am prepared to venture into the very depths if need be.'

Her courage shone from her glowing eyes, and we, her other daughters, knelt and offered worship. Had there ever been a goddess as gallant as Palu the Perfect?

The preparations necessary before we could actually set forth on our quest were many and demanding. The journey could prove arduous, so Palu insisted we train like athletes. We ate, we slept, we did exercises to build up our strength and stamina. There were sacrifices to be offered as well, and meditations required. We had to spend whole days without moving, opening ourselves up to the spirits of our ancestors and imploring their guidance. Even great Palu would not undertake such a journey without all the assistance she could command.

But at last all was in readiness. Through magical means which she never vouchsafed to us, our mother had located Tenya's trail and knew the direction she had taken. The news obviously disturbed her.

'That wicked, foolish child has gone straight towards our most deadly enemies,' she told us sorrowfully. 'Had she searched the entire world she could have found no worse a path to take.'

At these words Tinka gave a shudder of apprehension. 'Which way did she go, Mother?' she asked apprehensively.

'Across the River of Stone,' replied Palu sombrely.

This was grave news indeed. The River of Stone was the boundary separating Palu's world from a land where she had much less power, and one of our earliest prohibitions had been against crossing that petrified river. Even Tenya had not dared it — until now.

But Palu would not be shaken in her resolve. And so, when all possible preparations were made, we set off toward that terrible borderland. I confess I had many misgivings and am sure my sister Tinka felt the same.

If Palu was afraid, however, she did not let it show. O splendid is the goddess!

Inspired by her courage, we warily approached the River of Stone. Its surface had an evil glint in the light of a pallid sun and the shimmering heat waves dancing in the air above it were tainted bitter and foul. 'Many of our people have died here over the years,' my mother reminded us. 'If you are to survive, you must do exactly as I say.'

I had no intention of doing otherwise.

I stayed as close to her as I could, and when she set her foot on the river, I followed her instructions so precisely that my own footprints covered hers. I did not sink into the depths as I had feared, nor was I swallowed up and turned to stone as I had imagined. Instead I negotiated that fearsome place safely, though my heart was pounding in my breast every step of the way.

Tinka came right behind me. She too survived the perilous crossing, and Palu congratulated us both afterwards. 'You did as I told you,' she pointed out. 'That is why you are alive.'

Before we left the vicinity of the River of Stone I turned back for one last look, just to savour my success. Then it was that I observed the river was not very wide, nor did I see anything on it that could hurt me.

Nothing at all.

But a new danger awaited us. The gentle, rolling landscape we knew, with its lush woods and pools of sweet water, gave way almost at once to a barren desert. The smell of the desert made our nostrils burn. 'Poison land,' Palu informed us. 'I know spells to counteract the poison, but we must not linger here for very long. No matter what you see, do not fall behind.'

Her advice was sound. No sooner had we entered the desert than one wonder after another appeared, arousing our curiosity. So exotic were the features of this unfamiliar landscape that we surely would have succumbed to their enchantment, had not Palu warned us. 'Do not stay any longer than you must,' she kept repeating. 'One moment too many and you will be bound to this place, unable to leave; the poison in your lungs will chain you here, because you will not be able to breathe anywhere else, not ever again.'

And so, with resolute tread, we strode past the flowers of fire and the bridges of light, the silver spires and the golden globes. We did not pause to admire the miniature whirlwinds that danced toward us, nor did we turn aside to investigate the velvet caverns that exhaled an almost irresistible perfume. Nothing could tempt us, not with the words of the goddess singing in our ears.

When we finally left the desert my nose was still burning, and my eyes felt gritty and sore. but I had no real trouble breathing, in spite of what Palu had said. The stench of the place had done me no harm after all.

That first night we made our camp on a hill over-looking a valley of stars. We were weary, but Palu was tireless. While we slept she kept watch with all her weapons at the ready - many and terrible are the weapons of Palu! - and when we awoke shortly before dawn we found her sitting just as we had seen her in the last light of evening, with her head erect and her eyes unblinking. I had no doubt but that she had watched over us through the dangerous night.

Before we set out again, Palu provided us with a most sumptuous meal. After the manner of goddesses, she could conjure up food where none seemed to exist, and we heartily enjoyed the repast, which she had caught and killed and prepared herself. 'Eat every bite,' she commanded us. 'Listen to what I tell you: you will need your strength.'

Each day of our lives, in accordance with the ritual our mother had taught us, we had a period set aside for prayer. It was not always the same time of day, but was always of the same duration, an interlude of calm when we closed our eyes and bowed our heads and spoke with Palu in our inmost hearts. Even on this dangerous journey, we kept the faith and observed the ritual.

But for the first time, I found myself wondering with whom Palu spoke during prayer-time. If we prayed to the goddess...who then did the goddess pray to?

Once we were underway again, I ventured to broach this subject with our mother. Palu halted abruptly and looked at me in astonishment. 'You question me?'

'Not at all,' I hastily assured her. 'I was merely curious. Is there another deity even greater than yourself? If so, should we not pray to it as well as...'

'There is no deity greater than I!,' our goddess exclaimed in outrage. 'Who told you to ask such questions?'

'This is a thought I had on my own,' I replied, then added contritely, 'and I am sorry if it offended you.'

'So you should be, talking heresy like that.' Palu gave a delicate sniff. 'Oh, I know there are some misguided folk who claim Tall Ones are gods, but I can assure you they are not. They are worse than the Longtooth Demons, fouler than They Who Smell. They can even command the Great Dragon to their will.'

'Tall Ones?' said Tinka curiously. 'Who are they? You never mentioned them before.'

'And for a good reason, my daughter. I did not want to discuss Tall Ones until you were mature enough to understand. They are not nursery terrors, but the worst of our enemies, cruel giants who have deliberately murdered many of our people. Yet strange to relate, in spite of their terrible record some of our folk continue to fall under the influence of Tall Ones and defend them, even worship them.'

My sister gave a shudder of horror. 'Are there any

Tall Ones around here?'

'They are everywhere,' replied Palu. 'I have kept you well away from them so far, but we are in their territory now and going deeper with each step. If my worst fears are confirmed, your foolish sister has wandered into their very heart.'

I gave a gasp. 'How are we to rescue her if they are as bad as you say? Is this land not outside your sphere of magic, Mother?'

She gave me that wise, knowing little smile of hers. 'No land is ever entirely beyond my magic. If we find your sister, I feel confident we can rescue her. If she is still alive.'

Those last words chilled me.

Step by step, we advanced. I observed a change in our mother's demeanour, now that we were so close to Tall Ones. Always graceful, she seemed to glide when she walked with a movement so delicate and feminine that she melted into the shadows. Unless you knew exactly where she was, you would not notice her.

Tinka and I did our best to imitate her, but we were not goddesses. Compared to Palu, I fear we were clumsy.

Tall ones may have seen us.

The land of Tall Ones was a most peculiar place. Until I actually saw it with my own eyes I would not have thought any beings would choose to live as they did. They had an addiction to noise which I found frightening; they dwelt in a constant cacophony. Surely they could not hear the birds sing, nor the rustling of the trees' dance; I doubt they could hear their own thoughts, if they had any.

Because Palu had warned us, I was not unprepared for my first glimpse of Tall Ones... but even so the sight of them repulsed me. I found them singularly ugly and repellent, extremely awkward and they stank of a thousand bitter odours. Their gestures were abrupt and brittle, and they breathed with a great roaring noise. I think they could not have been very healthy.

They were strong, however, as a result of their hulking size. 'Whatever you do, never get within reach of one,' our mother warned us in her most severe tone. 'They can seize you and break you almost without effort. They like to break things: they are monsters.'

They were indeed monsters. I watched from the shadows as they went about their incomprehensible affairs, scurrying here and there for no reason, baying and screeching at one another, their ugliness equalled only by their clumsiness. 'How can anyone mistake them for gods?' I asked our mother.

'There are those,' Palu replied sadly, 'who are overwhelmed by their sheer size and assume that anything so large must be magnificent. I have also heard that Tall Ones employ traps baited with seductive luxuries. Some of our people mistake this bribery for generosity and give their fealty to Tall Ones in return. To justify this greed on their part they try to pretend Tall Ones are noble and fine, worthy of their loyalty. But it is a pathetic self-delusion.

'Tall Ones have no appreciation of our ancient culture. They use our people for their own amusement, as if they were clowns or court jesters. They mock our manners and degrade our dignity, and any form of relationship with them is a debasement.

'Never be fooled by Tall Ones,' Palu concluded. 'They are no good. I tell you this.'

Trying to be as inconspicuous as possible, we drifted through the kingdom of the Tall Ones. They tend to live in clusters, in hives, which makes the noise they create even louder and more disturbing. Indeed, I do not recall a single one of them alone in meditation, simply enjoying Being.

Palu has taught all her followers that To Be is the first imperative.

We searched for a number of days for our missing Tenya. Palu kept an optimistic attitude, at least for our sakes, but I suspect she was beginning to lose hope. I noticed that her appetite faded and the light in her eyes was less brilliant than of old. Her very step seemed duller and heavier. In my heart I wept, for the diminution of a goddess is a terrible thing.

Great Palu, queen of goddesses!

For fear of Tall Ones, our mother did most of her searching at night. Tall Ones are blind in addition to their other faults, and night rendered us all but invisible to them, whereas our night vision is legendary among the lesser races.

Our mother always tried to find us a place to hide up during the hours of sunlight, but sometimes the dawn caught us still going about our rounds. It was on one such occasion that we got our first clue to Tenya's whereabouts.

We were skirting a conglomeration of Tall Ones' hives - noisome, odiferous dwellings - from whence issued the awful roaring which Tall Ones make in sleep. I could see from the tension in Palu's face muscles that she was fighting back her revulsion, nostrils pinched tight, eyes almost closed. But she was determined to search every quarter for Tenya.

And then it was that she caught that first, delicate wisp of sound which could have issued from no Tall One's throat.

It came again, soft, plaintive...unmistakably the sound of one of our race, undeniably the sound of our sister. In spite of herself my mother gave a glad cry. Emotion washed through her, leaving her quivering all over, great tremors running the length of her body.

I pressed forward audaciously and kissed her. 'It's all right, Mother,' I whispered. 'We are with you.'

She relaxed then. 'My good and dutiful daughters, I did not doubt it for a moment. We share this joyous discovery. I tell you, she who was lost is found!' She returned the happy caresses Tinka and I were showering upon her, kissing our faces, our eyes, our lips. Great is the affection of Palu, and honoured its recipients!

With my mother's sweet breath in my nostrils, I regretted my earlier disloyalty. Obviously there could be no questioning of her wisdom; had she not found Tenya?

For there was now no doubt it was Tenya's voice we heard. Clear and pure as crystal, it rose above the ugly noise which marked the habitat of the Tall Ones. She was calling from somewhere nearby.

But where? We looked at one another in puzzlement. Although the voice sounded quite close, it was curiously muffled and gave no indication of direction.

Palu narrowed her eyes. 'They have her trapped,' she said bitterly. 'Tall Ones have captured my daughter, and are holding her a prisoner inside one of their filthy cells.'

I looked past my mother to the grotesque and massive hives of Tall Ones. The structures presented a solid face to the outside world, with no obvious way to get in — nor to get anyone out. The goddess read my mind. 'There are always entrances...and if Tenya cannot get out, we must get in to her.'

I bowed my head and nodded, unwilling to even think the blasphemous thought...that Tenya might not want to escape!

She had now been a captive of Tall Ones for some days. And Tenya was intelligent, there was no denying it. Surely she had managed to learn something of her captors, to discover their weaknesses and formulate some plan for her own escape? Surely, she had made a bid for freedom.

Led by Palu - the wise and wondrous! - we made our cautious way around and around the clustered hives, seeking an opening. Tenya's voice appeared to follow us, moving around the inside as we circled the outside.

At last Palu took a chance. After first glancing warily to the left and the right, she darted forward and flattened herself in an angle of one of the walls of the hives. There she began calling Tenya by name, using a low but penetrating tone her daughter must surely recognise.

Within moments she was rewarded by Tenya's voice answering from just on the other side of the wall.

Palu looked towards us. 'This is the place! Come!'

We ran forward eagerly and added our voices to our mother's. 'Tenya! Where are you, how are you? Can you get out?'

'I am here,' our sister replied. To my surprise, she did not sound as glad as we were. 'What are you doing here?' she asked rather peevishly.

'We have come to rescue you,' Palu replied.

'Rescue me? From what?'

'Tall Ones, of course! You are in terrible danger, my daughter!'

'Danger? You must be joking! I am with friends. Friends,' she added rather spitefully, 'who appreciate me as you did not.'

Palu reeled from shock. 'What are you saying?'

'I'm saying it was quite unnecessary for you to come after me. I am doing very well on my own, thank you'

'But...but we heard you calling for help...'

'Calling for help? No, you were mistaken. I was singing. My new friends enjoy my singing.'

Palu's jaw dropped. 'This is even worse than I feared,' she whispered to us. 'Your sister has gone mad.'

'What can you do, oh great goddess,' Tinka asked. Her eyes were wide with alarm.

Our mother was growing increasingly frantic. 'Something,' she muttered almost inaudibly. 'I must do something...'

She began to run around the wall of the hive. We followed her with our hearts in our throats, afraid that at any moment we would be discovered by Tall Ones.

But it was ourselves who made the discovery.

Rounding a corner of the hive, we found ourselves facing what appeared to be a huge opening. And Tenya could clearly be seen on the other side! Abandoning caution, Palu ran toward her daughter...only to smash against some invisible barrier that sent her staggering backward.

She shook her head to clear it and approached again, more slowly. We crept after her, unwilling to let our goddess face any danger alone.

On the other side of the barrier Tenya watched us with cold amusement. I hated her in that moment.

Once again Palu touched the transparent wall. 'What is this?' I heard her ask softly.

Muffled by the material, Tenya's voice replied. 'A door, Mother.'

'A door? Then come out.'

'I do not come outside any more.'

'What?' Palu asked in disbelief.

'Everything I need is in here, furnished by my friends,' our sister replied. She sounded so smug and superior I longed to slap her face. 'Look.' She gestured toward a bed piled high with soft cushions. Beside it a table was laden with quantities of food and drink. She lifted her sleek throat to display a collar with a tiny bell set into it. 'These are mine,' Tenya said proudly, her slave bell ringing softly. 'You have nothing so fine, living as you do by your wits.'

Palu gazed for a measureless time upon the luxuries Tenya boasted. Fine they were, and tempting; even I could see that. But I could also see the sorrow in our mother's eyes. They were filled with grief, as if she presided over the funeral of her beloved daughter.

At last she made one final plea to Tenya. 'If we can find a way to get you out, will you not come with us? Leave now, come home, before you are completely corrupted?'

Our foolish sister replied defiantly, 'I shall never leave!'

'Then we must,' said Palu. 'You think you have everything, my daughter, but I tell you this. You have surrendered your freedom, and so you have nothing.' Her voice turned bitter and contemptuous. 'You have dishonoured the race of Khat. You have become a...a *pet*.' To Tinka and me, she commanded, 'Come, my daughters.'

Resolutely, Palu stalked away. We followed her, shaken by what we had seen.

When we were a safe distance from the hive of Tall Ones, Palu paused and looked back one last time, calling her farewell to the cat who watched us from behind her glass door. 'You have nothing,' my mother reiterated, 'and someday you will realise it. Remember then: I told you so.'

Michael Scott

Liam Mac Uistin *has written many works in both English and Irish, and is another of these all-round types — he wrote both the moving inscription on the wall of the Garden of Remembrance in Dublin and the lyrics to Ireland's first Irish-language Eurovision entry,* Ceol An Grá. *This, it seems to me, is about as all-round as you can get.* Making Friends *is a chapter from a work in progress.*

MAKING FRIENDS

by Liam Mac Uistin

Young Timmy Galvin was the first to spot him. He was on his way home from school, walking slowly along the path that sloped up to his home perched on a hill overlooking Inishbeg Bay.

It was a warm day in early summer. Timmy unslung his schoolbag and sat on a rock to rest. He gazed down wistfully at the green Atlantic waves rolling into the inlet below. It was his favourite fishing place. He wished he could get his rod now and go fishing. But he'd lots of homework to do. He consoled himself with the thought that he'd soon be getting holidays and then he could go fishing to his heart's content. He sighed and stood up to continue his journey. Then he saw the dolphin.

It suddenly shot out of the water below, cleaved through the air and curved down under the waves. Almost immediately it arrowed into the air again, hung there for an instant, and knifed back into the sea. Timmy watched mesmerised as the dolphin playfully repeated its jumps over and over again.

The dolphin had a bottle nose and a happy grinning face. Timmy's face broke into a happy grin too. He whooped his appreciation of the performance. The dolphin responded with a high arcing leap. Then it swam in closer, rolled over on his side and beamed up at

Timmy with a large liquid eye. Timmy was about to clamber down to the water's edge when the dolphin turned suddenly and sped away through the waves.

Timmy waited for it to reappear. When there was no sign of the dolphin returning he grabbed his schoolbag and ran up the path. He burst excitedly into the house.

'I've just seen a dolphin!' he announced to his mother.

'Timmy, you're imagining things again,' she smiled.

'Honestly, I saw him in the inlet below. He jumped and dived and did all kinds of fabulous tricks.'

'Last week you thought you saw a whale and the week before that a shark. God knows what you'll imagine seeing next.' She put a plate of food on the table. 'Sit down now and have your meal. Then start your homework.'

When he had finished eating, Timmy took out his schoolbooks. But he found it hard to concentrate on the sums and spellings. He kept thinking of the dolphin, wondering if he would ever see it again.

As soon as his father arrived home Timmy told him about the dolphin. Mr Galvin shook his head in disbelief.

'No dolphin has ever appeared that close in the bay,' he declared. 'It must have been some other kind of creature you saw.'

Timmy was annoyed that his parents did not believe him. Next day at school he told his friends about the dolphin but they also refused to believe him.

But that afternoon the dolphin was seen again. A fishing boat was making its way back into Inishbeg harbour under noisy flocks of herring gulls when a torpedo-like shadow appeared beside it in the water.

'Look at what's following us, Shaun!' the crewman shouted to the skipper.

Shaun Cahill went to the side of the boat and glanced over. The dolphin was on the surface now, keeping pace with the boat. The crewman grabbed an oar and raised it menacingly.

'I'll soon send that thing off about its business!' he growled.

'No, leave him alone!' Loreto Garcia came running from the stern of the boat. 'Don't let him hurt him,' she appealed to Shaun.

'Leave him be, Mosheen,' the skipper ordered.

'But he'll interfere with the fishing,' the crewman protested. 'It's bad enough as it is without having him around.'

'Maybe he'll bring us luck,' Shaun said, rubbing his stubbly chin. 'God knows we could do with it.'

He glanced at the meagre catch of fish lying in the bottom of the boat. The days were long gone when fishing boats returned to Inishbeg stacked up with their catches. The once-prosperous little town was now in decline. It tried to eke things out by catering for the occasional tourist like Loreto but it wasn't easy to survive.

Shaun and the Spanish girl had become firm friends since the day she arrived on the harbour wall and asked him to take her for a trip on his boat. His first inclination was to refuse because he didn't want any people aboard who might get in the way. But he liked the cut of the sixteen-year-old girl with her pretty smiling face. Mosheen hadn't been too happy about having her aboard but his attitude changed when he saw that she knew her way around boats and enthusiastically shared in the work.

As Shaun took the wheel again Loreto whispered, 'Thank you. I think it would be wrong to harm one of those lovely creatures.'

Shaun nodded. 'Sure, haven't they as much right to be here as we have?'

'I wish everyone thought the same way as you.' She moved to the side of the boat and looked into the water. 'He's still there.' She stretched her hand out to the dolphin. 'He nudged my fingers!' she laughed. Then as the boat approached the harbour the dolphin suddenly turned and swam out into the bay.

'Maybe he will bring us luck after all,' Shaun said as he steered the boat towards the quay. 'If he stays,' he added.

Liam Mac Uistin

Morgan Llywelyn, *as well as her thriving international career as an adult writer, has written many well-known books for young people. Her book* Brian Boru *won the Best Emerging Author category in the Bisto Book of the Year Awards in 1991,* Strongbow *won both the Historical Fiction Award and the Readers Association of Ireland Book Award in 1993, and her book* Cold Places *was shortlisted for the latter prize in 1997. Her adult epic of the Easter Rising,* 1916, *is currently a bestseller.* Fletcher Found *was shortlisted for a Nebula Science Fiction Award, and is now unavailable.*

FLETCHER FOUND

by Morgan Llywelyn

Born a fletcher, I. A maker of arrows. Born light-boned and longmuscled into a tribe of knotty, barrelchested smiths and squat, sinewy miners, I had no choice but to learn the less strenuous art of fitting feather to shaft in order to support myself.

My people lived in the cold and arid mountains far above the Galzar Pass, wresting a precarious living from holes they gouged into the earth and raw materials they shaped into the weapons men always seem to require. Ours was a homeland of blowing granular ice and icy granular wind, and my people had long been numbed into bitter subsistence and nothing more.

But they were not really my people. Even as a small child I suspected it. My place was not among head-bowed, backbent folk who grovelled in front of traders, and snarled at one another over a few coins.

Does every child think he has been raised by the wrong parents, shipwrecked among strangers? Or perhaps not born at all, for the old women told no tales of my mother's labour, and never spoke of Weenarin as having been a red and mewling infant. So into this place by another route I had come. But from where? And how could I find my way back?

Then one season, just as my first beard started to itch, a trader told me the citypeople's legend of Three Lordly

Sky Ones who had descended to earth in a silver dwelling from the stars, and been hailed as gods. Good and kindly gods, incredibly clever and capable of stunning feats of magic.

Lightboned and longmuscled, that was how the trader described the Three Lordly Sky Ones. And when his words touched my ears I knew at last who I was. Whose foundling.

The Sky Ones had landed at Ithkar and subsequently vanished from there, leaving a riot of legends behind to be celebrated each year at the great fair which had sprung up around the earth scorched by their appearance. And in my heart I knew they had left one of their own behind them, a descendant born but for some reason unclaimed - stolen, perhaps. Lost in some tragic way before they returned to their starhome. Yet surely the Sky Ones knew of that child's existence and were watching for him with the infinite wisdom of gods.

Must get to the place where they had last been. Must find a way to signal to them, to summon them back for me!

Kept this knowledge to myself, I did, because the others would tease me cruelly if I whispered a word of it. But from that day I planned to go to Ithkar, and when my chance came I took it gladly. The year had been harder than usual, and traders scarce. There began to be talk of sending some of our wares to the great fair, for we had need of many things. Stout leather for boots, and potions for sickness, and even I needed a replacement for the piece of glass I screwed in my eye to allow me to study the exact angle and set of feathers as I affixed them to the arrowshaft, for the one I had inherited from my predecessor was cracked. It is no easy thing to be a good fletcher and give an arrow wings.

Begged to be allowed to go to Ithkar, I did. No one else was anxious to be scorned and spat upon as mountainfolk were in the lowlands. He who called himself my father scowled at me from under the thorny overhang of his eyebrows. 'For what purpose go you, Weenarin? Ithkar is far away and the journey is dangerous. Smarter men shrink from it, stronger men than you.'

Still I persisted, and at last they gave me an ass with a pack of tools and weapons strapped upon her back, bows and my arrows to sell, daggers, links of chain, hammers. And I faced into a howling wind and headed down from the mountains.

No one came out to bid me goodbye. That was their way; I understood.

The journey was even harder than I had imagined. The ass was stubborn and smart and made me manytimes angry, but I kept going. Below the Galzar Pass we came upon a metalled road with signposts I could not read. Miners and smiths are not allowed bookteachers; cityfolk do not want them to be wise. But stopped other travellers along the road, I — merchants and pilgrims to the shrine at Ithkar. And asked directions, and was told.

Told which fork of the road to take, where to pay tax or toll for crossing some border no one could see, what magics were prohibited at the fair. All of this was on the signposts, but someone had to tell me

'Do no magic, I,' I protested. 'My tribe would not live at the farthest reaches of misery if they could do magic.'

Was not even sure what magic was, but knew I had never done it. Had no intention of doing it at the fair.

Before I had half-completed my journey a band of nomads set upon me and cuffed me about, laughing, until they tired of the game and took the best contents from my pack and most of my food. Good daggers, they took, and axeheads too. They left me with nothing to sell but some bronze arrowheads they had over-looked, and no payment but the memory of their hard fists and kicking feet. 'Troll from the mountains,' they called me, not knowing who I really was.

Could have gone back to the mountainpeople and told of the robbery, they would not have been surprised. But then I would never have got close to the Lordly Sky Ones. So slogged on and on, dragging my beast with her depleted pack, searching for something to eat and something I could sell to earn admittance to the fair.

We eventually came to a marshland of still water and waving grasses, and there I let the ass graze while I daubed mud on my wounds. Hungry I was, and growing desperate, when a flock of birds flew in over the marsh. Great grey creatures with long necks and voices of haunting sweetness. In the mountains, a fletcher takes his feathers from hawks. Never had I seen birds such as these, with such plumage. It seemed to me that killing one would be a monstrous thing, though mountainfolk would not have thought so. Kill or be killed was their simple law. But I saw beauty in these strange grey birds and mourned in my heart, even as I tore one from the air with a stone in an improvised sling.

The bird lay at my feet, stunned and dying. It

stretched out its long neck and rolled one glazing eye upward, looking for its killer. My heart leaped with pity. Dropped to my knees in the mud, then, and tried to find its wound, tried to undo what I had done. But the bird was already departing on another journey and I could not hold it back. My tears fell upon it as my hands explored it with more gentleness than I had known I possessed, but it uttered one soft cry and went limp. In dying, it had extended its wings to their utmost so I could see the fine quills, the gloss and perfection of each feather. And I swear the bird was still watching me when the light went out of its eyes.

That night, beside my campfire, I skinned the bird and cooked its flesh, though I had little appetite for it. But I carefully cleaned the feathers and set them aside, and the next morning found me hard at work, making arrows from the wood of young trees which grew at the fringe of the marsh. Fletching the arrows with the feathers of the great grey bird. Sniffling a little, like a weakling, because so much beauty was dead.

The mountain tribe would have scorned me, had they seen.

When I had a sizeable bundle of arrows I looked at them with pride. No shafts had ever been so true; no feathers had ever been set more evenly. Took the only bow my assailants had left me, a poor thing with little power to it, and tried one of the arrows. It went straight for a target so distant I could hardly see it, and I found it dead centre there, though everyone knows Weenarin is an indifferent archer.

But the astonishing thing was the flight of that arrow. It sang all the way, a melody of great beauty such as the birds had sung in their flight.

When at last we neared the region of the fair my ass became nervous, which was a new thing for her. She stamped her feet and rolled her eyes, and when a gilded wagon with curtained sides passed us enswirled in dust my beast bolted, dragging me after her a goodly way.

Someone laughed behind the wagon's curtain. Laughed at me, not knowing who I was. Rippling, mocking laughter, unmistakably feminine — and though I had never heard such a sound in the arid mountains, I recognised the voice of wealth and privilege.

At the gateway I was halted by a condescending guard, who eyed my person with contempt. He seemed about to deny me entry until he picked up one of the arrows I held out to show him. He turned it over and over in his hands, staring at it, and I swear he began humming a pretty tune, deep in his throat. Took a step backward, I, thinking he might be going mad. We saw much madness in the cold mountains. But he looked up and met my eye.

'What, you still here? Why haven't you taken your place?' He caught my shoulder and held me like a child while he pinned a badge on me, then directed me to a distant cluster of merchants' stalls on the borderline between the area reserved for food and clothing and that for armourers and metal workers.

A shabby fletcher could not expect a stall of his own, but I was allowed to tuck myself and my goods into one corner of a canvas lean-to shared by a mercer and a pair of identical twins, two wizened crones who sold salt in leather bags. Tall, bony women who said I might tether my ass behind the tent.

The mercer was a spindleshanked, potbellied man with a walleye, but there was no meanness in his voice. 'This is a good location,' he assured me, 'though our pavilion isn't as fancy as some. But you should do well here. What's your name, lad?'

No stranger had ever asked for it before. Mountainfolk do not speak of themselves, nor hand out their names like gifts.

Then I remembered: the laws of the mountain tribe need not apply to me.

'Weenarin,' I told the tentholders in a bold voice, not bowing my head.

'What kind of name is that?' asked the mercer, mopping his domed forehead with a square of fine fabric.

One of the old women pressed forward. She had wispy grey hair and more gaps in her mouth than teeth; her eyes were as bright as a ferret's. 'A mountain name,' she told him. 'This fellow is dressed like the trolls from the mining district; a strange people, surly and...'

'They're not my...' I began, but then I swallowed my words and my secret. The old crone seized my words like a terrier seizing a rat. 'What's that?' she said. 'You're not from the mines?'

Lowered my eyes then as I had been taught all my life though pretending inferiority burned me like fire. 'From northern mountains, I come,' I muttered.

The mercer shrugged. 'That's an end to it then.'

'No, wait,' said the second crone. 'There is something about this fellow. I cannot imagine him standing over a forge, or wielding a pickaxe.'

'Fletching is my trade,' I said, willing to give them that much.

'Shoot one of your arrows for me,' suggested the mercer. 'If I like your wares I might buy some myself. We do a bit of hunting where I come from.'

My one remaining bow was not very impressive, but I responded to their kind interest and let them put up a target in the weedy lot behind the tent. By the time I set arrow to bowstring a small crowd had gathered. People at a fair will crowd up for anything.

Felt the weight of judgement in their eyes. They saw how slender my arm was and doubted my ability to send an arrow more than a short, erratic distance. But when I held the arrow and saw the grey feathers sleeking back from the shaft, I deliberately moved back from the target, so many paces that someone snickered, 'The lad has delusions of grandeur.'

Set my feet and braced my body; drew my elbow straight back in line with my ear. And arrow left bow with an exultant hum that became winged song as it flew.

The onlookers gasped. Shaded my eyes against the sun and tried to see the target, but it was too far away to be certain. Trotted forward with the crowd, and when I arrived men were already pointing it out to one another. 'Dead centre!' 'An incredible shot!'

'An accident,' said a different voice, a hulking, flat-faced man wearing the uniform of a fair-ward. He carried a weighted quarterstave and his eyes were constantly shifting, alert for trouble. He jerked the arrow from its target and handed it back to me. 'Shoot again, boy,' he ordered. 'There are three explanations for such a shot — accident, skill, or magic. From the looks of you I doubt that it's skill. If you are illegally using magic to glamourise your wares we had best know it now. The fair-court deals harshly with such trickery, it will cost you your goods and you will be declared outlaw, driven out of the gates and thrown to the mercy of the people. And I warn you, mountain boy, the people of Ithkar are not noted for their compassion!'

Driven from the gate. Denied access to the shrine of the Three Lordly Sky Ones before I even had a chance to see it. That was a far worse threat to me than mere outlawry, for mountainfolk were treated little better than outlaws anyway and were used to it.

'His arrow sings a strange song in flight,' someone in the crowd murmured. 'I heard it, and I say it must have been magic.'

'Shoot!' roared the fair-ward, doubling his fist at me.

'Do no magic, I!' I protested. But how could I keep the arrow from singing, or flying true an impossible distance? The magic was in it and not myself, though by now I was certain of its existence. Certain of it and doomed by it.

They made me stand where I had stood before, too far away for any normal shot to succeed. My heart hammered at the base of my throat as I notched arrow to string. Could have pulled the shot, of course, and let it fall short, for my skill was enough for that at least. But when I held the grey-feathered arrow a sort of integrity moved from it into my hand, and I fired the best I could.

The arrow arced up, up into the air, climbing as if it spurned the earth forever. Then suddenly it bent in its flight and coursed off to one side, toward the gathered crowd. In helpless horror I watched as it sank straight into the shoulder of the fair-ward, in the joint his breast-plate did not cover.

He yelled and clutched at the shaft. 'Now you've done it,' the mercer said to me in a low voice. 'If you run quick, you might make the river before they seize you...there are caves there where you could hide...'

Running I was, but not to the river. Running toward the crowd and the fair-ward, as if my feet had a will of their own. For beyond that shouting throng of people was the shrine, and if I was to be exiled or killed I would at least see it first, somehow.

But when I drew near the fair-ward I found an astonishing thing. He had pulled the arrow from his shoulder, and in spite of the good bronze head I had affixed to it my weapon had made hardly any wound. A little blood oozed, then stopped as if the skin closed up. And the man was smiling!

Stopped still and gaped at him, I.

'That was a clumsy shot, young man,' the fair-ward said, handing me back my arrow. The head was still warm where it had been heated in his flesh. For some reason I thrust it through my belt instead of putting it back in my quiver. 'You're too thin to be a bowman,' the man went on, 'you need fattening up if you're going to be able to demonstrate your wares impressively. Here...'

He dug into a pocket and took out a fistful of coins, which he pressed into my astonished hand. 'Go to the food stalls and buy yourself a decent meal, will you? And then get some clothes that look like something, we can't have beggars in rags at the fair, it isn't good for business.'

He grinned at me as if I were his dearest friend, and then turned his back on me and began breaking up the crowd, calling names, punching noses, threatening to break heads if they did not move along. A fair-ward, surly and short-tempered.

What to do? Took the money and ran, as fast as my legs could carry me. When I had gone far enough to be out of his sight I opened my fist and found more coins than I had ever seen at one time before.

It appeared I could do some sort of magic - or magic could do me, since I had no control over it. That was yet another proof of kinship with the Lordly Sky Ones, was it not? And now I was very near the place where they had entered this world. Soon I would be standing just where they had stood...

Stuffing the coins into the little leather purse which had hung from my belt like an empty bladder until now, I headed toward the sacred precincts

Felt the hackles rise on the back of my neck. No one needed to tell me where the sky-descended dwelling had rested; even without the fenced-off enclosure and the reek of incense and the muttering of priests I would have known the place. Needed no stone cenotaph to guide me. Would have found it by the lines of force surging up from the ground, catching my feet and drawing me forward.

Surely this was the heart of the universe, the place of perfect centredness. As I drew close to it I felt myself on the verge of a breakthrough into unimaginable abundance. At this point the Three Lordly Sky Ones had achieved immortality by becoming gods to us. And wherever they had gone, in their infinite and godlike wisdom they must be aware of me. Would surely reach out and gather me in, now that I was here. Would lift me up . . .

'Stop that, you beggar, what are you doing here?!' Harsh hands grabbed me, pinioning my arms behind my back. Angry faces surrounded me. Eyes were flashing, mouths were stretched wide with yelling, but I hardly heard. Kept concentrating on the Sky Ones, calling desperately to them to come back for me, feeling almost confident, almost safe, for the first time in my life. Had got so far against such odds, I.

Then someone hit me a mighty blow on the side of the head and I tumbled off the world.

When I woke up, I was lying in a stone cell bedded with filthy straw and slimy refuse. No head ever hurt worse than mine. The room was dark and stinking, worse than any mountain hut. Shut my eyes tight and willed myself to be somewhere in the silvery vault of the sky with my true people. When I opened my eyes again, however, I saw only a scruffy rodent no more than a handspan from my face, watching me with dispassionate assessment.

Sat up abruptly and the creature scurried back, but not very far. A quick inventory of myself showed they had taken my purse, my bow and quiver - but somehow overlooked that last arrow, the one I had thrust through my belt. My ragged tunic must have concealed it.

If I possessed magic, this was the time to prove it —

and legally too, for was this not self-protection? Flung my arrow straight at the rat, like a killing-dart. Saw it hit the mangy hide and bounce off harmlessly, falling into the straw.

Where was the magic?

On hands and knees I crept forward and reclaimed my only weapon, while the animal watched me. In dark corners, his littermates chittered and rustled the straw.

Footsteps on stone in the corridor, and the heavy door grated open. Someone thrust a lamp into my cell and an old woman hurried forward to bend over me. The door was shut behind. Even in the dim light I recognised her as one of the twins, the salt peddlers from the fair.

'You're accused of invading the shrine, Weenarin,' she said in her cracked voice. 'It's a serious charge, the priests want you executed. Is there anyone you can send for who will pay for your freedom?'

Pay for my freedom. The mountainfolk? No, I had no resources with fat bribes in their pockets. I had nothing at all. It seemed even the Lordly Sky Ones were not interested in me. That had been a childish fantasy, I saw now; this prison cell and the hungry rats were the reality.

She saw my shoulders slump. 'I thought not, lad. You must do for yourself, as we all do. You are alone among strangers.' An odd look flitted among the wrinkles of her folded face, and she dropped her voice to a whisper. 'Alone as the Lordly Sky Ones were when they arrived here, no doubt, and had to depend upon their wits and skills to survive.'

My face must have mirrored surprise, for she cackled a laugh. 'Did you think they just sank to earth and were immediately hailed as gods? How little you know of life, Weenarin! Don't you suppose it more likely they met a hostile reception at first? Judge by your own experiences. They were strangers and very different from the natives; they were probably attacked and captured, imprisoned maybe, and had to disguise themselves very cleverly in order to escape. And then the authorities, to cover their embarrassment at being outwitted, may have surrounded the advent of the Sky Ones with all sorts of supernatural tales which became myth and miracle in time...' She clamped her jaws on her words like a trap snapping shut. Instinctively, I understood the danger there must be in telling tales so at variance with the dogma of the priesthood.

The old crone leaned closer to me, thrusting her face into mine until I shrank back, which made her laugh again. 'You think I am ugly, Weenarin? This wrinkled old visage displeases you?'

Kindness curved my tongue. 'Your face is the map of your years,' I told her. 'The landscape of a life is an honour to its wearer.'

She straightened up. 'Come,' she said briskly. 'It is time to leave this place.'

'But how? I am imprisoned for a crime — will they just let me walk out of here?'

'Of course not, no one ever lets anyone do anything. Just bring that arrow and follow me.'

Set in the door of my cell was a narrow window, high up, just large enough for the face of a guard to peer through. The old salt peddler went to this door and knocked, and when the guard looked in she told him,

'I'm through now, let me out.'

'Is this a relative of yours after all?' the guard asked. 'Will you pay for his release?'

She snorted. 'Of course not, he's a mere nobody from the mountains. I was mistaken.'

The bolt was drawn and the door swung open just enough to let an old woman walk out; a tall, gaunt woman wrapped in a voluminous cloak. She did not wait for me or offer any suggestions.

A slender fellow, crouched down, could almost hide himself in her shadow. Made my decision and scurried after her, squeezing through the doorway with her body between me and the guard, shielding me. The corridor was almost as dark as the cell had been, and we had left the lamp behind on the straw. The guard did not realise what had happened until we were several paces beyond him. But then he let out a yell that would bring skeletons out of their graves.

The old crone darted forward, carrying me in her wake like a whirlwind. There were men rushing after us, but she dodged this way and that, down twisting passages and through narrow openings I never noticed, but the old woman found unerringly. Like rats in their warrens, she seemed perfectly familiar with the dank stone fortress where I had been imprisoned. She knew it better than any of our pursuers, in fact, for when we at last emerged from some abandoned storeroom into a courtyard overgrown with brambles, there was no one behind us. Far off, I could hear the ringing of alarm bells, but we were free.

Wanted to express my gratitude to the old woman, but she shrugged it off. 'The oppressed learn many skills,' she said. 'And sometimes we are able to use those skills to help a fellow creature. It is nothing, only common decency.'

Common decency. Never before had I heard that phrase, and it went into me like an arrow.

In the clear light of day I could see that she was very pale and her breathing was laboured, and I felt guilty for having put an old body to such strain. But she refused to rest. She set off in a westerly direction without looking back, and I trotted like a dog at her heels because I had nowhere else to go anyway.

'How will you care for yourself now?' she asked after a while. 'Your goods were confiscated.'

'In my bedroll - which was poor and shabby and not worth taking, I hope - I still have a supply of the grey feathers I used to fletch arrows,' I told her. 'If I can get them, surely I can find wood for shafts. My bronze arrowheads are gone, but there is flint in the hills and I know how to chip it into arrowheads if necessary.'

She turned and looked at me, and her eyes twinkled in their network of wrinkles.

'You have a fallback position, I see. I like that, it speaks well for your thought processes. There is a deserted farmstead not too far from here where you may hide, if you like, while I return to the fair. Salt must be sold, business must be done - you understand. My sister and I can send you a little food, later, and we will get the mercer to see if he can find your bedroll and feathers. If you are fortunate no one has bothered with them.'

'Never been fortunate, I,' was my reply. A miner's son, no Sky-Born princeling. But then I thought of the grey feathers and the singing arrows and bit my lip. Thought of the old woman and her brave kindness, and regretted my words.

That night I lay shivering in a half-collapsed cow byre, hidden from the nearest road by a stand of woods but close enough that I could hear the clatter of hooves and the frightening sounds of what might have been a search party, looking for an escaped prisoner. Sometime before dawn I finally fell into a troubled sleep, and when I awoke the wall-eyed mercer was standing over me, with my bedroll tucked under one arm and a pail of broth in his hand.

He watched in amusement as I gulped down the soup. 'I've forgotten what an appetite a growing lad has,' he remarked. 'It's been so long...'

When my belly was as tight and round as his, I put down the empty pail and wiped my mouth on my sleeve. He had squares of fine linen for mouthwiping, but he did not offer me one. 'Now that you're fed and have your belongings, such as they are, I must leave you,' he told me. 'I must be getting back to the fair.'

Back to the fair. Rested now, and a little less afraid, I too yearned to go back to the fair! To stand for just one moment more at the sacred shrine and feel the sweet glory roiling through me; to believe myself to be part of something splendid instead of a mere troll from the mountains, outlawed now and futureless as well. But I said nothing of this. Pride was strong in me and would not ask for pity.

Perhaps that is why he hesitated before leaving me there. If I had asked for help, would he have abandoned me? Will never know, but sometimes I wonder.

'Weenarin,' he said at the entrance to the byre, with one foot already out into the sunshine. 'I've been thinking. You have a skill, and - perhaps - some small gift for magic, though I confess I do not know exactly what sort of magic it is or how used. I cannot take you back to the fair with me, for you would be arrested on sight and I as well, for harbouring you. But in less than ten days the salt peddlers and I will be returning to our own valley, many days distant from here.

'We are not much bothered there by the authorities, the sheriffs and tax assessors and their ilk. It is a pleasant place, but those of us who live there have to work hard to maintain ourselves. You know how to work hard though, don't you?'

Nodded. Could not trust myself to speak.

'Very well then. If you can continue to hide yourself successfully until it is time for us to pack up and leave, you can come with us if you like. We can use a good fletcher. We don't offer you more than you're willing to get for yourself, you understand. But the only other option you have is to try to get back to the mountains, and that would be a hard journey for a lad alone, impoverished and with a price on his head.'

This was not the choice of my dreams, the radiant beings in their silvery palace, holding out a hand to their true son and asking forgiveness for having left him behind. Offering luxury, offering godhood. No. Nothing I had come to the fair expecting had happened as I imagined it would. Instead I had been robbed, imprisoned, and brushed with an odd touch of magic over which I had no control. And now I was offered a life of continuing labour among strangers in a strange place.

No Sky-Born lordling, I — and I sneered at myself for ever thinking otherwise. The mountains which had made my tribe hard and bitter had failed in their duty to toughen me; had left me with a burden of compassion for injured birds and old women. So probably I should not try to return there; was not fit to live among stronger folk.

That is how Weenarin came to be in this caravan heading west, muffled to the eyes in a salt-peddler's cloak, carrying a heavy load of fabric bolts belonging to a potbellied mercer. In my bedroll lie the grey feathers, sleek and shining, and when we reach the distant valley I will make arrows and put them into the service of these people who have befriended me.

Do not know what I can do for them; do not know if the very arrows I make may not someday turn against me, for they have a strange power beyond my understanding. But at least I will be with three friends who are not bitter by nature, though they are as ugly as I am, a scrawny mountain troll. And mayhap I will grow to be content in their company. Though not happy; I do not expect to be happy, since I am not who I dreamed of being.

Born a fletcher, I.

Larry O'Loughlin *is Aislinn's embarrassing father—no home is complete without one. Apart from his writing Larry is a tireless and welcome visitor to schools around Ireland, where his storytelling delights many children and (even) teachers. His collaboration with John Leonard,* The Gobán Saor, *was shortlisted for the Bisto Book of the Year Award in 1998.* The Great White Stag *is published here for the first time.*

THE GREAT WHITE STAG

by Larry O'Loughlin

The old stag moved slowly towards the white cross. He was tired now and too weak even to hold his antlers high. With each step his body ached a little more.

Surely his time would be soon.

The little buck walked beside him, his eyes filled with excitement and pride to be walking at the head of the herd with his grandfather.

At the foot of the cross, the old stag lay down. The buck lay beside him, resting his head against the great body. The herd lay down in front of them in a half circle. As they lay there in the soft moonlight the old stag closed his eyes. He was breathing heavily, and the pain in his neck was growing stronger. This park was the only home he had ever known. Surely, he would be leaving it soon.

Soon, his time would come.

The young buck nudged him with his nose. 'Grandfather, please tell us one of your stories. Tell us of Lord Eraglinn, the Great White Stag.'

The old stag opened his eyes. Each face in the herd was turned towards him. He smiled gently.

'What I tell you now is true, as true as I sit before you.' His voice was soft and warm. He cleared his throat and began:

'The Lord Eraglinn, the Great White Stag, was walking slowly along the western shore. The cool waters of the ocean flowed gently over his feet. It was here the Great Lord came when he wanted to be at peace. When he wanted to remember the times of long ago, when the great herds roamed free and the three islands that stood proudly in the distance had been part of the land — his land.

'They had been times of joy and freedom. Then came man.

'MAN!

'The Lord Eraglinn, the Great White Stag, hated even the sound of the word.

'MAN!

'With his spears and axes, his swords and his arrows, what had man done to the land?

'He had fenced and divided the plains, scarred the valleys and hills with his ugly tracks and roads, destroyed the rivers and fouled the lakes and streams.

'Then, for his own sport and pleasure, man had hunted the great herds, and worn them down until all that remained were the lame and broken few.

'All this the great lord saw.

'Suddenly Lord Eraglinn, the Great White Stag, lifted his head and sniffed the air.

'MAN!

'He could smell man coming towards him.

'Once, a long time ago, he had enjoyed the chase, but now... Too many ages had passed, and he wearied of their game.

'Could they not see that he, who could leap from the Northern Highlands to the Southern Lakes in five steps, would never fall to them?

'He listened. The sound of their yelping hounds, their thundering horses and their hunting horns came closer.

'Would they never leave him alone?

'With one leap he was on the cliffs that looked out onto the islands. With another he had travelled over many counties to land on the flat-topped mountains. A third took him home to his beloved Northern Highlands.

'All day he wandered the streams and the valleys, his heart heavy with thoughts of the past. When night fell, he climbed to the highest peak and called to his creator to show him a place where he might find peace once more.

'Suddenly a light surrounded him. It was a golden light so bright that for a moment he was blind. Then, as his eyes grew accustomed to the light, he saw ahead of him a path. It was a path of golden leaves that stretched far out into the skies.

'The Lord Eraglinn felt a new feeling. He did not know what it was.

'Could this be the thing they call fear? he asked of himself

'He held his head high.

'"I am the Lord Eraglinn!" he said. "I am the Great White Stag!"

'Slowly at first, then more quickly, the Lord Eraglinn rode out along the path. On and on he journeyed until he came at last to a place where the waters sparkled, the birds sang, the sun shone and the grass grew sweet and tender. Here was a place where the great herds could roam once more - free of man.

'From that day, none in this land has seen the Great White Stag until his time has come. Then the great Lord comes to bring him home.'

The old stag stopped. He looked from the herd to the young buck and back again. 'And on that day,' he said, 'each will be as strong and as well as a two-year-old buck or...' - he smiled at the buck - '... as this little pest here beside me.'

The herd laughed.

'And now, my dear friends, we must rest.'

The old stag closed his eyes. Soon the field was filled with the gentle peace of sleep.

The little buck was the last to close his eyes. For some time he lay and looked up at the stars and thought of the golden path and of Lord Eraglinn, the Great White Stag. But then even he drifted off, with the warmth of his grandfather beside him.

When he woke it was still dark. He felt cold and frightened. He didn't know what had woken him, but it wasn't nice. His heart was beating fast. He turned to call his grandfather, but the old stag wasn't there. The young buck jumped to his feet and looked wildly around. The rest of the herd lay still sleeping.

Across the road, at the edge of the wood, a shadow moved slowly, unsteadily towards the trees. It was the old stag.

'Grandfa...'

The buck stopped. It would be unfair to wake the others with his shouting. He crossed the road and ran to the edge of the woods. His heart was still beating fast.

'Grandfather?' he called softly. 'Grandfather?'

There was no reply.

He called again.

'Please answer me, Grandfather.'

There was still no reply.

The young buck looked into the trees. It was so dark there that he could see only a little way.

'Please, Grandfather. I'm afraid.'

There was still no reply, and the little buck stood frightened, staring down the dark path in the trees.

The Lord Eraglinn had also once been faced with a strange path.

Step by step, inch by inch, the little buck began to move forward into the darkness. He was too frightened to call out now, and he was almost too frightened to move. The darkness swallowed him here. It surrounded him. Still he moved forward.

Then he saw it. A light. At first it was so far away it looked no bigger than an acorn; but the closer he came, the bigger it grew. The bigger it grew, the faster he moved. First he walked quickly, then he trotted, then he galloped. Then he was in a clearing, and the light was there too.

In the middle of the clearing, his grandfather lay on his side. He was perfectly still.

The young buck nudged him gently with his nose. The old stag didn't move. The buck licked about the face and eyes. The old stag lay still. He felt cold, colder than the little buck had ever known him to feel. He licked his Grandfather again. He nudged him in the neck, in the stomach.

'Grandfather, Grandfather, wake up,' he pleaded. 'Please wake up. Let's go back to the herd, Grandfather. Please.'

'HE MUST COME WITH ME NOW, LITTLE BUCK.'

The little buck spun around. At the edge of the clearing, just a few steps away, stood the most noble stag he'd ever seen. He was tall and white, straight as a young oak, and his giant antlers shone like pure silver.

The buck backed away, and gently nudged his grandfather with his rear leg.

'Grandfather! Grandfather!'

'HE MUST COME WITH ME NOW, LITTLE BUCK.'

'No!' shouted the little buck wildly. 'No!'

He turned and started licking and nudging the old stag frantically.

'Grandfather! Wake up! PLEASE!'

'HE MUST COME WITH ME NOW, LITTLE BUCK.'

The buck spun round angrily to face the stranger. 'You shan't take my Grandfather!' he said. 'You shan't! You shan't!' He dropped his head to a fighting position, pointing imaginary antlers at the great stag.

The stag smiled fondly.

'Come, little buck,' he said. 'Come to me. Come to me now.'

The little buck didn't want to move. He wanted to stay where he was, guarding his Grandfather. But slowly, very, very slowly, he felt himself drawn to this great stag. The white stag lowered his neck until their heads were almost touching.

'Little buck, I see well the love that you have for your Grandfather. But there is a time when we must love not as a child but as one grown. For you, that time is now. You have seen your Grandfather grow old and weary, and so full of pain that he could hardly hold his antlers high. Is that what you want for him? Or would you want more?'

As he spoke, the great stag breathed softly on the little buck. The buck felt the warm perfumed breath fill his body. He looked deep in the stag's eyes. Somewhere, outside the two of them, the woods, the stars and the heavens seemed to float past.

'I ask you again, little buck: is that old, frail body what you would truly wish for your Grandfather? Or would you wish more?'

The great stag lifted his head and stepped back. The young buck blinked in astonishment. He was no longer in the clearing. He was standing instead on a hill of soft, sweet-smelling grass. Below him in a river meadow were deer - more deer than he'd ever seen or even imagined, deer more numerous than the stars in the sky. Along the river, up in young, firm mountains by a waterfall's pool the great herds roamed, rolling and laughing and running free, while above them birds sang sweetly.

'But it's beautiful!' sighed the little buck. 'So beautiful!'

'And all this awaits your Grandfather,' the great stag

said softly. 'Many of those that you see here were far older and weaker than he when first they came here. Would you deny him this, little buck? Would you?'

The buck slowly shook his head.

'No,' he said. 'But I will miss him greatly'

'No more than I will miss you.'

The buck turned his head. Two young stags walked gracefully towards him.

'Grandfather? Is that you?'

The leading stag smiled.

'It is!' said the young buck. 'It is you!'

He bounded across and nuzzled and licked at his grandfather's neck.

'Oh, Grandfather! You look so well! You look so young and happy!'

'As I always shall be in this place. I will feel no weakness here, no pain. Here I can wander all day with the great herds, and never need to rest. Here...' he paused, and looked at the young buck. 'Here is where I belong now. Please be happy for me.'

Tears filled the little buck's eyes.

'I will, Grandfather, I will. I'll be happy for you but ...'

He turned his head to hide the tears.

'But I will miss you so,' he said.

'And I will miss you, little buck...and someone else will miss you too: has missed you already.'

'Hello, little buck,' said the second newcomer.

The little buck stared at him. Did he know him? He knew he'd never seen him before, yet somehow the stag seemed familiar. A strange tenderness came over the little buck as he looked at this stag. His heart beat fast again, and his body trembled.

'I'm your father, little buck,' the stag said.

'Father?' The little buck's voice trembled too. 'My father?'

He could speak no more. Tears rolled down his cheeks.

His father licked the tears away, and nuzzled the little buck's head.

'Yes, little buck. Your father. Even though I lost my life to one of man's road machines before you were born, still I have loved you. And oh, how I've missed you.'

And then no-one spoke. There was no need for words. Father and son, Grandfather and Grandson nuzzled against one another in the warm, sweet breeze.

When at last the silence was broken, it was the Great White Stag who spoke.

'Little buck, it is time to go back.'

The little buck was startled.

'So soon? Can't I stay?'

The white stag spoke softly.

'When your time has come, then you'll return. On that day I will come for you. And on that day too your Father, and Grandfather - and many you have yet to meet and love - will all be waiting here for you to meet. On that day, little buck, you will know the joy of running with the great herds — free of man. But until then...'

'But...' said the little buck. 'But...'

The Great White Stag breathed on him with his warm perfumed breath. The little buck's eyes closed and he felt himself drifting away. And even though his eyes were closed, still he could see his Father and Grandfather running with the great herds, while the Great White Stag watched over them from the hillside.

A strange, whining noise filled the little buck's ears. He opened his eyes. He was in the clearing in the woods. His own herd was there. They were looking down at his Grandfather's body, and they were crying. The little buck sat up. He looked at each sad face in turn, as the first light of morning filled the clearing.

'Don't cry for my Grandfather,' he said. 'He has gone with the Lord Eraglinn, to a place of joy and beauty.'

'Do you know of its beauty?' asked an old doe.

The little buck nodded. 'I do.'

'Will you tell us about it?' asked his mother.

The little buck smiled. 'I will, if you wish.'

The herd lay down. Each turned to face the little buck. He smiled gently. He cleared his throat.

'What I tell you now is true,' he said. 'As true as I sit before you.'

His voice was soft and warm when he began:

'The Lord Eraglinn, the Great White Stag, was walking...'

Larry O'Loughlin

Siobhán Parkinson *has written nine books for young people. Her novel* Sisters, No Way *won the Bisto Book of the Year award in 1997, while* All Shining In the Spring *was shortlisted for the same prize in 1996 and* Amelia *in 1994. She is also the author of* Four Kids, Three Cats, Two Cows and One Witch (Maybe), *which was chosen for the White Ravens series by the International Youth Library and won a Bisto Merit Award in 1998.* Snake *is an unpublished story for young children.*

Marie-Louise Fitzpatrick *is one of the only three holders of a Bisto Book of the Decade Award (1980-90) for her book* An Chanáil, *which also won the 1989 RAI award. She also won a Bisto Award in 1992 for her book* The Sleeping Giant. *Her 1998 book* The Long March, *a story of the Choctaw Indians' contribution to famine relief in Ireland in the 1840s, was one of the most highly-praised Irish publications of 1998.*

SNAKE

by Siobhán Parkinson

Nobody loved
    Sidney.

Willa the woodpigeon was
wary of him.
Egbert the hedgehog turned
nasty when he saw him com-
ing.

Hatty the cat
hated him.

Even Plato the tortoise
tucked his head and feet in
and pretended not to be at
home when Sidney slunk by.

'Poor me,' sighed Sidney sadly, slithering softly home. 'Nobody loves me.'

'Pull yourself together, son,' Sidney's dad ordered sternly, as Sidney snivelled to himself.

So Sidney tried to pull himself together, but he hadn't got the hang of it just yet.

'Never mind, Sidney,' said Sidney's mother soothingly from the tree where she was sunbathing. 'Come and curl up here with me.'

So Sidney did.

It was good to be home.

Once or twice Sidney almost made a friend.

One day he met a small animal with a big tail.

Sidney tried to help it out, by combing its big bushy tail with his forked tongue.

But it seemed the animal didn't need any help. As soon as Sidney started combing, the small animal's mama came bustling along, chattering and complaining, and threw nuts at Sidney, till he slid away silently into the grass.

And once a very strange animal appeared in the garden. It didn't have any fur, except on its head, and it couldn't walk or slither or climb or jump. It just sat there on its puffy little bottom, babbling and gurgling to itself, and banging strange coloured objects together. But when Sidney went and introduced himself, the funny new animal started to wail for its mother.

So Sidney snuck off home before the animal's mother got there.

Another day, when Sidney was sloping along a sunny branch, he found a beautiful oval pebble in a twiggy little basket that was perched among the leaves. He thought, If I can't have an animal friend to talk to then maybe I can just make friends with this nice smooth pebble here. It's better than an animal who hates me, anyway.

But just then a raucous robin came flapping and screeching at him, and poor old Sidney had to slip away. He never saw the pebble again.

Sidney just hung about after that.

He gave up going down the other end of the garden, where the woodpigeons and the squirrels and the hedgehogs and the robins lived.

And he kept well away from the house, where Hatty the cat lived, and the strange animals with fur on their heads.

He stayed at his end of the garden, where nobody ever came to call, and tea was always just family.

But Sidney soon got tired of just hanging about in his own end of the garden. He decided one day that he would pay a little visit, just the littlest one, to the other end of the garden. So Sidney set out bravely to see what he could see.

He saw the small animal with the big tail scurrying about under a walnut tree.

Sidney waved, but the animal was too busy to notice
him.

He saw the strange animal with fur on its head sitting
in a very odd-looking little tree, all of its own.

He waved, but the strange animal just stared at him.
He saw the robin digging for worms.

He didn't like the look of this, so he didn't wave.

And then he saw Hatty the cat, sitting under a tall, tall tree, and staring right up into its topmost branches.

She was concentrating so hard on looking that she took no notice of Sidney, even when he sidled up quite close and stared up into the treetop too.

Swaying on a branch, high, high up in the tree, was a tiny black smudge.

As Sidney stared, the smudge mewed.

A kitten !

Oh my, thought Sidney. It's stranded.

He looked at Hatty and wondered why she didn't rescue her daughter. Scared of heights, he thought. Oh well.

And without giving it a moment's further thought, Sidney started up the tree.

When he reached the top, he hooked his tail around the topmost branch, where the kitten was, and stretched and stretched till his head reached the ground.

The clever kitten understood at once. A slide!

She sat on Sidney's tail and whee! - down she slid to the ground and landed at Hatty's feet.

Hatty picked her kitten up in her mouth and shook her good and hard, to show she was annoyed with her.

Then she dropped her on the grass and licked her good and hard, to show she loved her.

And then Hatty turned to Sidney and bowed, to show she was grateful to him.

Sidney bowed back solemnly, and then he slid away about his business, grinning broadly to himself, and occasionally coiling and uncoiling his tail, just for the fun of it.

At teatime the next day, the kitten Sidney had rescued came bounding along and landed in a small round heap

at the tea-table and promptly fell asleep.

Then Hatty the cat came slinking by, pretending to look for her kitten. When she saw the kitten all curled up asleep, she sat down beside her as if she was waiting for her to wake up, but really hoping somebody might notice, and offer her a saucer of milk.

Sidney's mother looked from the cat to the kitten and back to the cat again, wondering what they were doing in this part of the garden.

Then she looked at Sidney, who was looking very pleased with himself.

She shrugged what would have been her shoulders, if she'd had any shoulders, and carefully poured a saucer of milk for Hatty.

Hatty gave a small bow and began to lap the milk up, as if she came to Sidney's for tea every day.

Sidney goes up the other end of the garden quite often now, to visit Hatty and her kitten.

Who knows, one day the robin or the squirrel or the tortoise or the hedgehog or the woodpigeon or maybe even the baby may come and visit Sidney's part of the garden and stay to tea.

In the meantime, Sidney's quite happy just to be friends with Hatty and her kitten.

Somebody loves Sidney after all.

In fact, two somebodies do.

And that's two better than nobody.

Gerard Whelan's first book, Guns of Easter, *was awarded the Eilis Dillon Memorial Award as well as a Merit Award at the Bisto Book of the Year Awards in 1997, and was shortlisted for the RAI prize in the same year. His second book,* Dream Invader, *won the Bisto Book of the Year Award in 1998.* Jailbirds of a Feather *is a story from a work in progress — or in this case, maybe a work in regress.*

JAILBIRDS OF A FEATHER

by Gerard Whelan

It had rained all night, but spring was in the air that Sunday morning as Tommy Harte wandered down towards the Grand Canal. The skies had cleared, and the sun had heat in it. The air was sweet with the smell of wet fresh greenery from the trees lining the canal. It was a springtime smell to gladden hearts after the winter's misery, but it had no effect at all on Tommy.

Only one thing in the world would have gladdened Tommy's heart, and that was his Da's release from jail. That wasn't due to happen for another four years. This fresh greenery would ripen, waste and die; three times after that these trees would bud and flower, then fall back again to winter bareness. Only then - if all went well - would Harry Harte come home. And until then his youngest son's heart would be as bare as any winter tree, and no sun mere would gladden it.

Tommy Harte's father had been in jail already for a year. He'd been sent there for taking part in the Easter Rising of 1916. It could have been worse, mind you: originally he'd been court-martialled and sentenced to death. That had been just after the Rising was crushed, when Martial Law was in force. A lot of people had been sentenced to death then: the military courts had been handing out death sentences, Granda Keane said, 'like snuff at a wake'. Fifteen executions had actually been carried out. Later, when things calmed down, almost all of the surviving rebels' sentences had been reduced. Harry Harte's death sentence had been cut to five years imprisonment.

Tommy didn't have a mother. She'd died when he was born. He lived now - he and his brother and sister - with Granda Keane, her father. Granda Keane kept a shop at the back of Westland Row. It was a small shop, in a poor area. It brought in enough money to feed the four of them, more or less, but sometimes they did go hungry. When things got too bad Granda Keane would use up some of the stock from the shop, though he hated doing it. 'Cutting rashers off the pig,' he called it. It was a saying he had. Granda Keane had lots of odd sayings, most of them pessimistic. Tommy's brother Patrick had asked him what this one meant.

In the old days, Granda Keane said, the poor tenant farmers would keep a pig. Meat, though, was a great luxury for them; they kept the pig to sell, so that they could pay their rent to their landlords. If they ate the pig, they'd have no money, and would be evicted. But sometimes, when families were almost starving, they'd eat the pig. It was a case of having to. Then they'd end up evicted, and would probably starve anyway.

'They were damned now if they didn't eat it,' Granda Keane grinned grimly through his thick white beard, 'and they were damned later if they didn't. But sometimes picking the time of your damnation is the most you can do in this life. It's some kind of choice at least.'

Patrick was good-hearted, but he wasn't the most quick-witted boy in the world. 'I still don't understand,' he'd said when he heard the explanation. 'How can we be evicted? I thought you owned this house.'

But Granda Keane had only smiled. 'Never mind, Pat,' he said. 'Sure it's only an ould saying.' And he'd given Patrick a lump of barley sugar from the big glass jar on the counter. Barley sugar took Patrick's mind off everything else, except maybe his desire to fight for Ireland as his Da had done.

But Tommy had understood straight away that Granda Keane wasn't talking literally. The profit from the shop was what they'd use to buy future dinners; if they ate the stock, they couldn't sell it later. Eating the stock wouldn't really cure hunger, only defer it to another time.

Tommy loved his Granda Keane. He loved Patrick too, and his sister Hannah. But he did more than just love his father: he worshipped him. He always had. 'Harry's shadow', Granda Keane used to call him, in the days before they'd all lived together. It wasn't meant unkindly, and Tommy had never felt offended by it. It was true, too, in its way. Tommy had never liked to be parted from his Da for long.

'It's only to be expected,' he'd heard Granda Keane say. 'The poor motherless child.'

Granda Keane loved all three of them, but there was something special in his love of Tommy. Sometimes Tommy would ask him about his mother, and Granda Keane would tell him stories of what she was like as a little girl. It reminded Granda Keane of his lost youth, his lost wife and daughter. Sometimes Granda Keane would end up with tears in his eyes when they talked: he was a daughterless father, just as Tommy was a motherless child. When those tears did come to his grandfather's eyes, Tommy looked away; the old man didn't like him to see them. His dead wife and daughter, and the dead who'd died for Ireland: these were the only things that ever brought tears to Granda Keane's eyes.

Since Da had walked out of the house to go fighting Tommy felt sometimes that he really was Da's shadow. The rebel prisoners were being held in England, and Tommy hadn't even seen his Da's face since before the Rising. Sometimes now he felt exactly like a shadow: a shadow whose owner had gone away. Nothing in the world could be as lonely.

It was still early in the morning, and the streets by the canal were almost empty. On the corner of Mount Street Tommy passed the gutted ruin of Clanwilliam House, the former rebel stronghold. The rebels there had taken a fearsome toll on a regiment of the Sherwood Foresters during the Rising, before being bombed out by grenades. The owners of Clanwilliam House, Granda Keane said, were having trouble getting compensation from the government to pay for rebuilding it. From the glories of rebellion to the haggling over money was a big step, Granda Keane said.

'It's two different worlds, lads,' he'd say to Patrick and Tommy. 'The sublime and the ridiculous. And never the twain shall meet.'

Across the street, at Mount Street Bridge, Tommy left the road. There was a towpath by the canal here, below the level of the street, leading towards Baggot Street Bridge. At this early hour it was a fine and private place for a boy wanting to be alone with his feelings.

Tommy left the bridge and walked slowly along the towpath. Sometimes, like this morning, his loneliness got on top of him. He'd sit in a corner without the energy even to be sad. He'd want to do nothing except, very badly, to cry; but that would seem like weakness, and he'd try to argue himself out of it. Was it all right to cry? It was the sort of question he'd have asked his Da, but his Da wasn't there. Tommy didn't trust anyone else enough to ask them. They might think he wasn't proud of his Da, and he was — he just missed him, that's all.

'Are you in a mood, Tom?' Hannah would ask when she noticed how quiet he was being. Hannah was never sad, or at least she never showed it. She'd chatter and joke, trying to cheer him up. Patrick would just give out to him.

'Pull yourself together,' he'd say. 'Da wouldn't like to see you like this. Don't let him down.'

'Hush,' Granda Keane would tell them. 'Lay the child alone.'

And being left alone, until the mood passed, was all that really worked. Granda Keane seemed to understand that, but Hannah and Patrick didn't. Tommy didn't like letting them down, so when that mood took him he'd go out. He'd try to find a quiet place, so that if the urge to cry took over then at least no-one would see. Today the mood was bad. It was the end of April — the first anniversary of the Rising. And last night, again, he'd dreamed about Da.

The water in the canal was dark and still and silent. You couldn't see the bottom, only the reflection of the sky. When Tommy was almost halfway to Baggot

Street Bridge, something plopped gently into the water from the bank just in front of him. He caught a flash of brown, but it was gone before he had a chance to register what it was. A rat, he guessed. There were lots of them here. He stopped to look, but saw nothing now except the gently spreading ripples on the water. He shivered: he hated rats.

There was a movement in the undergrowth to his left. A cat appeared and meowed at him. It was too sleek to be a stray. A household cat, impatient for its breakfast, out hunting. Maybe it had been stalking the rat in the water.

'Did I ruin your hunt, cat?' Tommy said. 'I've nothing for you. But there'll be plenty more rats along here.'

The cat heard the gentleness in his voice. It came over, purring loudly, begging. It rubbed hard against his legs, the way cats do. Tommy, for no good reason, was suddenly disgusted by it. In a flash of bad temper he kicked the animal roughly away from him and walked on. After a few steps he stopped and looked back. The cat was sitting there looking after him. He knew cats had no expressions, but still he imagined that this one looked offended. Its look rebuked him.

'I was just being friendly,' it seemed to say.

Tommy walked back and crouched down in front of it. He held out a hand. Delighted, the cat rubbed its head and body fiercely against his clenched fist.

'I'm sorry, cat,' Tommy said. 'Sure we all needs a bit of affection.'

Tommy wasn't a rough boy. Sometimes he worried that he was a bit of a sissy. He longed for the days when he used to sit on Da's lap, with Da's arms around him, feeling safe. Hannah hugged him sometimes now, when she saw him looking sad, but it wasn't the same. Granda Keane, though affectionate in many ways, just wasn't the sort of person who went in for hugs. And Patrick, though he was fond of wrestling, thought hugs were definitely sissy things. Da's hugs had smelled of tobacco and soap and ink, and of the warm human mixture of smells that was Da. They'd smelled of warmth and love and safety from the whole world. And then that world had taken them away.

Whenever he dreamed about Da now, Tommy always dreamed of smelling Da's smell. One time it had seemed to linger faintly even after he woke. When he'd realised it was only a dream, Tommy had started crying straight away. He'd hated himself for that: it was a soft thing to do.

'Sorry cat,' piped a mocking voice from above. 'Sure we all needs a bit of affection.'

Tommy, startled, looked up. Something cracked on the path by his foot and bounced into the water with a plop harder than the rat had made. A stone. A second, better aimed or luckier, hit the hand that was stroking the cat. The cat was gone so suddenly that Tommy didn't see it move.

Tommy's hand stung where the stone had hit it. When he glanced at the hand he saw a graze. He peered upwards. The towpath here was maybe ten feet below the roadway, and the stones had come from the road. Tommy saw two faces looking down at him through the railings that bounded the footpath up there. The faces were grinning stupidly. Bigger boys. Tommy recognised one of them as Jiggers Quinn. His father owned a pub. Jiggers' real name was Timothy, but he was called Jiggers because that was his father's name. He was twelve years old, but he was in Tommy's class in school. The teachers called Jiggers stupid, but really he just couldn't be bothered learning anything. He enjoyed bullying the smaller children, and Tommy, like the rest of them, stayed out of his way.

Tommy had seen the other boy around, but he didn't know his name. He knew he was from Sandymount, like Jiggers, and he'd heard someone say that his father was in the Dublin Metropolitan Police. The DMP had never been exactly popular, but in the changing political mood since the Rising they were looked on by some now as little more than agents of the British. People said that it was DMP detectives who'd picked out the rebel leaders for execution. That had not made them popular.

'Little Tommy Harte,' Jiggers Quinn said. 'The jail-bird's son.'

He and the DMP man's son laughed.

'Do you need a bit of affection, little rebel Tommy?' Jiggers jeered.

The policeman's son swung his arm. Tommy realised he was pegging another stone, but hadn't time to react. The stone hit the side of his upturned head. His cap took the worst of the impact, but Tommy was dazed by the sheer unexpectedness of the blow. He stumbled and fell on the grass, hearing the rough laughter from above.

'Another rebel down!' he heard the DMP man's son call. 'Another blow for King and country!'

'Come on,' Jiggers Quinn said. 'Let's go give him his bit of affection.'

Tommy was still half-stunned, and his head hurt where the stone had hit him. But he knew that if these two caught him he'd feel a lot worse. They'd beat him up just to amuse themselves. It was their idea - probably their only idea - of a good time. He made himself get up. His cap had fallen off, but he didn't stop to look for it. He couldn't see the others now, but he could hear their running feet. They were making for Baggot Street Bridge, from where steps led down to the walkway. More importantly, Tommy realised, they were *both* making for Baggot Street Bridge. If each had gone a different way then they'd have had him trapped: there would have been one of them at each end of the towpath, and he could have escaped them only by jumping into the canal. Now he still had a chance. Maybe the teachers were right: maybe Jiggers really was stupid.

Tommy took to his heels. He was a small boy, and not strong; but he could run better than anyone he knew. He ran for the next bridge down. He didn't look back. Behind him on the towpath he heard the pounding of two pairs of boots.

'Come back here, Harte!' called Jiggers Quinn. 'Take it like a man. You know we'll get you anyway!'

Maybe they would, Tommy thought; and then again, maybe they wouldn't. He wasn't that far from home, but he doubted that he could outrun his hunters all the way there. He was fast, but he was a sprinter: he couldn't keep up the speed. His best bet now was to get to the other bank of the canal, putting the water between himself and the other two. If he could use his speed to get far enough ahead then they'd never catch him. They were only doing this to amuse themselves; they'd get bored with the game soon enough if it didn't go their way. They were probably just mitching Mass - it was the only reason he could think of that they'd be up this way so early on a Sunday morning. When he risked a look over his shoulder he saw that his pursuers were dressed in their Sunday best. Jiggers Quinn's unruly hair was smarmed flat by hair-oil, and shone in the sun. Mitching Mass: definitely. Jiggers had no business in a church anyhow: bullying was his true religion.

Tommy's heart was pounding, and he was frightened, but his mind was clear. The glance back had shown him that he had some hope of outrunning the pair. They were gaining on him, but there was still a good distance between them. He had almost reached the bridge.

Something smacked on the path at his heels: Jiggers or the DMP man's son had paused to pick and throw another stone. That was good: it was nearly an admission that they didn't expect to catch him.

Tommy's feet hit the roadway of the bridge, still running strong. Behind him the pounding of the others' feet sounded closer, but still not close enough to catch him. He would be on the wrong side of the canal now, with his hunters standing between himself and home; but they'd have to go away sooner or later — especially if they were supposed to be in church. Mass would end in less than half an hour: surely they'd have to leave then.

Maybe even that wouldn't matter. If Tommy was away for a long time then Granda Keane would send

Patrick to look for him; and if Patrick saw someone bullying his little brother then they'd be in big trouble. Patrick and Tommy were very different, and they didn't always get along; but with Da away Patrick saw himself as the defender of his family. And if there was one thing Patrick loved, anyway, it was a good fight. The bullies were Patrick's size and age, and there were two of them, but he wouldn't worry about that. He'd go through them for a short-cut.

Tommy was nearly smiling as he reached the south end of the short bridge and turned down by the canal again. He felt a crazy urge to laugh. There was something terribly exhilarating about just running. A glance showed him that the others were still on the far bank. They were still running, but more half-heartedly. Jiggers Quinn stopped and cursed at Tommy, shaking his fist at him. They weren't far apart, but the distance between them was mostly under water. Tommy felt confident enough to stop for a moment. His lungs felt like they were bursting. He gasped in air, but made sure to smile at Jiggers Quinn.

'Did you want me for something, Jiggers?' he panted.

He never saw the DMP man's son throw the stone. He never even saw the stone itself, but it must have been a fairly big one. It hit Tommy squarely in the middle of his forehead. He saw a sudden great flash of light, and then he saw nothing at all.

Tommy shook his head. He was lying on his back on the ground. There was a pain in his head, and he felt something wet on his face. His mind felt very fuzzy. He knew he had to get up and move — fast; but he wasn't sure why.

There was the sound of boots, running, growing closer. Two young voices whooped with empty-headed glee. Tommy opened his eyes and saw Jiggers Quinn and the DMP man's son closing in on him. His head was suddenly very clear, though it still hurt. He felt at the wet on his face and then looked at his hand: it was smeared with blood.

The stone, he realised, had knocked him out for a few precious seconds: only a few seconds, but too many for his own good. The hunters had crossed Mount Street Bridge and were almost on top of him. He wasn't going to get away.

Then Jiggers Quinn stood over him, red-faced and panting.

'Hello there, jailbird,' Jiggers said. 'You fell down.'

There was a sneer in Jiggers's voice. The DMP man's son, a roly-poly boy, rolled up and stood grinning stupidly, gasping. He had a round, puddingy face. It was even redder than Quinn's, and his gasps ended in wheezes. His face was smeared with freckles.

'Croppy lie down,' he said, and giggled.

It was threatening to have two people standing over you like that as you lay hurting on the ground. It was even more threatening when one of the people was Jiggers Quinn. The DMP boy had a way with stone-throwing, too, that did nothing for Tommy Harte's confidence in the boy's good nature.

'What'll we do with him, Eddie?' Jiggers said.

'With a rebel's boy?' the other said. He pretended to think. 'We can't shoot him,' he said. 'We've no guns.

And we haven't a rope to hang him. It's a real poser, Jiggers, my boy.'

'We'll make him sing *God Save The King*,' Jiggers Quinn suggested.

There was an air of emptiness off the two boys that disgusted Tommy. You often saw it in bullies. A sort of cow-like, unthinking air. Not thinking, Da always said, was the biggest sin: it was the sin for which there was no forgiveness. And as for God saving the King, well... a year ago now the whole centre of Dublin had been flattened by the King's soldiers, in the King's name. Tommy's father was in jail in the King's name. Their King had taken his Da.

'I'll sing *God Save The King*', Tommy said angrily, 'when the king takes his bloody soldiers out of my country. And his bloody police as well.'

He grew cold listening to himself speak. His words were asking for trouble; and these two were just the sort of people who'd give it. Giving trouble was what they did best.

For a moment the boys stood looking stunned by Tommy's cheek. Then, acting as one, they bent and pulled him roughly to his feet. Tommy struggled, but he was helpless in their rough grip. The DMP man's son, Eddie, slapped the back of his head.

'That's a nasty looking cut you have there, jailbird,' Jiggers Quinn said. 'Mind he don't get any blood on you, Eddie.'

Eddie slapped Tommy again. 'If he dirties my Sunday clothes,' he said, 'then he'll rue the day he ran into Eddie Griffin.'

Tommy was ruing that day already. His head still

hurt from the stone, and rang from the slaps. Each of the bullies held one of his arms tightly, and that hurt too. Why, he wondered, had he cheeked them? It would only make things worse. But, now that they'd actually caught Tommy, the two boys didn't seem to know what to do with him. They stood for a while, cuffing and cursing him, and made vague threats. But imagination wasn't their strong-point.

'We'll steal his clothes,' Eddie suggested finally, 'and leave him to walk home in his drawers.'

That was a bit too complicated for Jiggers Quinn, whose mind ran more to simple violence. 'Let's throw him in the canal,' Jiggers said.

The DMP man's son giggled. 'Aye,' he said. 'That's a good one.'

Tommy didn't share his enthusiasm. He twisted suddenly, wrenching one arm free from Jiggers Quinn's grip; but the other boy still held him.

'Get his legs, Jiggs,' Eddie Griffin said. And Quinn grabbed Tommy's ankles, though Tommy kicked fiercely. But it was useless to fight them: they were just too big. They lifted him, still struggling, and carried him to the water's edge. His struggles only made them laugh.

'You could do with a wash anyhow, Harte,' Jiggers Quinn said. 'You smell like a traitor. Ready, Eddie?'

'On the count of three,' the DMP man's son said. 'Right? Heave-ho — one... two...'

They swung Tommy, still trying desperately to kick free. On the count of three they both let go. Tommy flew threw the air and landed, with a great splash, in the middle of the canal. The cold of the water made him shout, but when he opened his mouth it filled with scummy water. He stood, spluttering. The water reached to his oxters. He splashed with his arms, feeling his coat grow heavier as it soaked up dirty canal water. Jiggers Quinn and the DMP man's son stood on the bank, almost staggering with laughter at their own cleverness.

'How about a bit of target practice?' Jiggers said. He bent and picked up a stone, then threw it at Tommy. The stone landed harmlessly in the water.

'You need something bigger,' the boy Eddie said, and looked around.

Suddenly a shout came from the direction of Mount Street Bridge.

'Hoi, there! What are youse doing with that kid?'

All three of the boys stared. A fourth boy, older than Tommy, smaller than the two bullies, was walking purposefully down the towpath towards them. He was comfortably dressed, but his body had the thin, wiry build of undernourishment. He looked angry.

'What are youse at?' he demanded.

'Mind your own business,' Jiggers Quinn said, but his voice was uncertain. The newcomer looked too confident. No bully liked confidence: it reminded them too much of what they didn't have themselves.

'Is it you, Jiggers Quinn?' the boy said. 'And Griffin, the spy's pup?'

A sort of scalded look flitted across the face of the DMP man's son.

'Who are you?' he asked. Being recognised by somebody he didn't know obviously disturbed him, not to mention the casual insult.

'His name is Conway,' Jiggers Quinn said. 'He should be all right — his Da is in the army.' Still he didn't sound entirely sure. The newcomer certainly wasn't acting 'all right'. Quinn gestured towards Tommy, who was starting to wonder whether he should swim for the other bank.

'This is only a little rebel,' Quinn said. 'His Da is in jail for the Rising.'

The new boy stood in front of them now, his hands in his overcoat pockets. He looked down at Tommy, shivering in the chest-high water. 'Maybe his Da knows my uncle Mick, so,' he said. 'He's in jail for the same thing.'

'This is none of your business, Conway,' the policeman's son said. 'We're just having a laugh.'

The newcomer had reached the two boys on the bank by now. He stood and looked in the DMP man's son's eyes. 'I don't,' he said, 'see anything funny. But then your family have a peculiar sense of humour.'

'What's that supposed to mean?'

'Your Da used to laugh and he breaking workmen's heads with his truncheon during the General Strike. I often heard me Da and the other men talking about it. A bad one, they said he was.'

'He was doing his job. And what of it?'

'Nothing. Only he didn't find it so funny when one of them broke his jaw, did he? One that saw him coming, like.'

The boy called Eddie flushed, whether from anger or shame Tommy couldn't tell.

'I know the man that done it,' Conway said. 'He said it was the greatest pleasure he ever got in his life. In fact he liked it so much that he said he must do it again sometime. He said your Da was easy enough to handle when he was on his own. Like any bully, really.'

Jiggers Quinn obviously felt that they were losing control of the situation, and wanted to get it back. 'None of us,' he pointed out, 'is on his own. Except you.'

The boy Conway shifted his stance slightly, but it was a significant shift. He stood straighter, his two legs planted slightly apart. He took his hands out of his pockets, and though he held them by his sides still he clenched his fists. Tommy, though he took heart at the sight, couldn't held noticing that the fists were small.

'I've been on my own before,' Conway said. 'And I was facing worse nor you two.'

'There aren't any worse than us two,' Jiggers Quinn said automatically; but you could hear that his heart wasn't in it.

The newcomer shrugged. 'I don't mind bleeding,' he said. 'They'll give out to me when I go home, but when I tell them how I got hit they'll be proud. What about you, Quinn? I suppose you're mitching Mass. Do you want to try explaining to your Da how you got bloody in a church?'

You could see that Jiggers, while no stranger to blood, didn't like thinking of spilling his own. Nor did he fancy explaining such a thing to his father. It was well-known that Jiggers senior beat his brood at the drop of a hat. Tommy had heard once, from a man who'd seen it, how the elder Quinn had sent Jiggers to collect some money from a family who'd owed it to him. When Jiggers had come back without the cash his father had knocked him flat with a box to the side of the head, right into the sawdust on the middle of the floor in their pub.

'I'll tell my father,' the DMP man's son said, 'that you're threatening us.'

'Your father,' the boy Conway said harshly, 'is a well-known cur; but he's not a fool. Tell him I threatened you because you attacked a Republican prisoner's son. Times have changed in Ireland, Master Griffin. Your Da mightn't mind you picking on this kid — but he'll mind you being seen. And my Da is in the army, like Quinn said. Fighting for your King and your country. He's won a medal for bravery, so he has, while your Da is skulking around taking bribes off publicans like ould Jiggers' Da here. That wouldn't sound very good, now, would it, if you had a go at me?'

The bullies were redfaced and frowning. Conway seemed full of ideas, and ideas weren't really their territory. He spoke, too, with a confidence Tommy admired. He'd no idea whether what the newcomer said really made sense or not — who, after all, would be interested in the doings of four boys by the canal on a Sunday morning? But it all *sounded* like it made sense, and it obviously troubled Quinn and Griffin.

Jiggers Quinn nudged the other boy. 'Let's get out of this, Eddie,' he said.

'I won't be bested by a little pup like this,' the DMP man's son said.

'My Da,' Jiggers said, 'is expecting me straight back after Mass. And it must be nearly over by now.'

The boy Conway stood watching them, but he said nothing. You could see that Griffin was as anxious as

Jiggers to be gone, but he didn't want to lose face. All three boys stood silent for long moments, watching each other. It was as though Tommy, still shivering in the water, wasn't there at all. Then a bell began to toll in the distance, from the church in Haddington Road.

'That's the bell for nine o'clock Mass,' Jiggers Quinn said nervously. 'Come on, Eddie, for God's sake. Don't dirty your hands on this little rebel.'

Tommy gritted his teeth, feeling the cold water soaking into his already sodden clothes. The DMP man's son shrugged and relaxed his stance. 'I'm going,' he said. He raised a finger and shook it in Conway's face. 'I'll see you again,' he said.

Conway smiled. 'I'm really afraid now,' he said. 'I'm wetting meself.' But he didn't sound afraid at all.

Jiggers Quinn pulled at the DMP man's son's arm. 'Eddie,' he hissed. 'Let's go. Me Da will kill me if I'm late.'

Griffin shook his hand away, but turned and stalked off towards Mount Street without looking back. Jiggers Quinn stood for a moment looking at Conway. Then he turned to Tommy and sneered at him. 'As for you, jail-bird's son...' he began.

'Shut it, you,' Conway said. Jiggers flushed. He wasn't used to being talked to that way. It was the other boy's confidence that frightened him. Only a true scrapper would dare to talk like that. Jiggers turned and left without saying anything more.

Conway turned, grinning, to Tommy Harte. He came over and stuck out a helping hand. Tommy waded over to the bank and took the hand gratefully. With Conway's help he clambered out of the water and stood dripping on the bank.

'Thanks,' he said, very sincerely. 'I'm Tommy Harte.'

'Jimmy Conway,' the other boy said. He stuck his hand out again. Tommy took it, and they shook hands.

'You're brave,' Tommy said. 'Would you have beaten them if they'd fought?'

Jimmy Conway's face lit up in a grin. 'You must be joking,' he said. 'I couldn't fight me way out of a paper bag. Me little sister can beat me up - though she's hard, mind you.'

'But then why did you butt in?'

Jimmy Conway shrugged. 'Sure I couldn't leave you there,' he said. 'Not with them two. Besides, I hoped it wouldn't come to a fight. Them boyos are cowards.'

'Like most bullies.'

'Aye. Where do you live?'

When Tommy told him, Jimmy frowned. 'You need to get out of them wet clothes,' he said. 'I'll tell you what.' He jerked his thumb over his shoulder in the direction of Mount Street Bridge. 'I live just over there. We only moved in lately. Why don't you come back with me and dry off there?'

'My own people might be wondering where I am,' Tommy said. 'My brother might be looking for me already.'

'Sure once you're in my house I'll go and tell them where you are. You really should get dry — you'll catch your death of cold.'

Tommy thought he'd caught cold already. The water seemed to have chilled his very bones. Water streamed from his clothes and formed a puddle at his feet. But the casual kindness and concern of the other boy had warmed him in a place that was much colder.

'All right,' he said. 'If it's no trouble.'

'Don't be thick. Of course it's not. Me Ma loves having someone to fuss over.'

A stone hit the path a few yards from them, and both boys turned to look. Jiggers Quinn and Eddie Griffin, feeling cockier with distance, were standing at the end of Mount Street Bridge. Both of them started pegging stones.

'Janey mack,' Jimmy Conway said. 'Don't they ever give up?'

The bullies were too far away to be very accurate with their stones, but they were blocking the direct route to Conways'. Jimmy sighed. 'Too thick to know when they're bested,' he said.

Another figure walked unto Mount Street Bridge, coming from the city side. The stone-throwers didn't notice him, but Tommy Harte did. 'That's my brother Patrick,' he said. 'Now we'll see something.'

Patrick Harte, deliberate as ever, stopped and looked at the stone-throwers. Then he looked to see what they were throwing stones at. Then he walked over and, without saying anything, hit Eddie Griffin a box in the head. From the canal bank Tommy and Jimmy saw the DMP man's son fall.

'Ouch,' Jimmy said. 'I'll bet that was sore.'

Jiggers Quinn turned to Patrick Harte and said something. Patrick made no reply that they could see - not in words, anyway. Instead he punched Jiggers in the stomach, and then in the mouth.

'That boy is a scrapper,' Jimmy Conway said. 'I

157

could feel them boxes from here.'

'He is,' Tommy said almost wistfully. 'I wish I was like that, sometimes.'

'I never do,' Jimmy said. He sounded serious. 'It's no way to settle anything. Come on.'

Quinn and Griffin were running away without making any effort to fight it out. Patrick stood looking after them calmly. After they were gone down Northumberland Road he came to meet his brother and his rescuer.

'They beat me up, Pat,' Tommy said. He was still dripping water, and had left a sorry trail behind him on the towpath. 'Then they threw me in the canal. They called me a jailbird's son. This is Jimmy Conway. He saved me. He bullied the bullies — he bluffed them.'

Patrick nodded to Jimmy Conway. 'Thanks,' he said.

'Jimmy's uncle is in jail for the Rising,' Tommy said. Relief was making him babble. 'He might know Da.'

Patrick nodded again. 'How long's your uncle in for?' he asked.

'Three years. Your Da?'

'Five.'

'That's rough.'

'It is. But he done what he had to do.'

'Aye.'

'You're not big. You were brave to stand up to them two.'

'But sure I only done what I had to do too,' Jimmy said. 'Us jailbirds have to stick together.' He looked at Tommy, still streaming water beside them, and grinned again. It was a nice grin, the sort that made you want to grin along. Wet as he was, Tommy felt himself cheering up.

'Jailbirds of a feather,' he said.

Jimmy Conway laughed. 'Jailbirds of a feather,' he repeated. 'I like the sound of that. Now why don't the two of you come to my house. We'll get Tommy dried off and I'll get me Ma to make hot chocolate.'

'I loves,' Patrick said, 'hot chocolate.' He did, too, Tommy knew; it was just that they didn't often have any chocolate, hot or cold.

'If I saved Tommy,' Jimmy said, 'then you saved me. You'll be filled up with hot chocolate in my house, Patrick. And the woman downstairs makes these great big cakes that she sends up to us. She sent one up last night. Fruit cakes.'

'Fruit cakes,' Patrick said. He was always hungry. 'Is there raisins in them?'

'Patrick,' Jimmy said, 'there's more things in Mrs Breen's fruitcakes nor I can tell you. There's fruit in them cakes, man, and I don't even know what it is - except that it's lovely, and there's loads of it.'

Patrick licked his lips. 'Well,' he said. 'What are we waiting for?'

And they set off back along the towpath, three boys, with the smallest one in the middle. And that smallest boy, although he still dripped and shivered, and though his shoes squelched with every step, felt suddenly warm and safe between the two bigger boys. It wasn't the same warmth and safety he felt in his Da's arms, but it was good. The broad shoulders of Patrick on his left, and the slim ones of Jimmy Conway on his right, were strong in different ways. And each of the two boys had used their different strengths to rescue him from the stupidity of the two bullies this morning. They were jailbirds of a feather, flocking together, and that flocking had a warmth all of its own.

Gerard Whelan

__Cora Harrison__ is the author of the Drumshee Timeline *books, partly inspired by the remains of an iron-age fort on her small farm in Co. Clare. This is all she wants said about herself, though I'm sure there's much more to say.*

DESTRUCT

by Cora Harrison

How could she do it? She didn't know. She gazed at
the broken bowl.

Every shard of splintered blue glass seemed to
accuse her.

'Perhaps it was the cat,' she muttered

Her mother did not even bother to answer, but turned
away. Her brother sniggered. Philip was always mean
to her. It had been a stupid thing to say, though; she
knew that now. No cat ever removed a solid glass bowl
from the window sill and flung it right across a fifteen
foot wide room so that it shattered into a hundred
pieces against the stone fireplace.

'You were the only one here, Caroline,' said Maria
gently. 'The rest of us were out all the afternoon.'

Caroline hung her head. Somehow she minded most
of all about Maria. She admired her sister so much. She
had always admired her and loved her and Maria had
always been kind, in spite of the five years' age differ-
ence between them.

'Perhaps Caroline was trying to see if it would look
better on the mantelpiece and then she dropped it acci-
dentally,' suggested Maria. Her stepfather looked
around with an expression of hope on his kind, slight-
ly silly face.

'No,' muttered Caroline. 'I didn't touch it. Honestly,

I didn't touch it.'

She looked around at all the unbelieving faces and burst into tears.

'If you would just tell us why you do these terrible things,' said her step-father gently. 'Just tell us, and then we will try to help you.'

Caroline shook her head and escaped to her bedroom. If only she knew herself. She was bewildered. She just didn't know why. There was no explanation. It would be all right for the next few days, perhaps even a week, she knew that. And then it would all start again. She opened her schoolbag and began to do her homework. Would her mother help her, she wondered. Or were things just too bad for that? She decided to try.

'Mum,' she called. 'Will you help me with my spelling?'

Her mother still looked very upset when she came in. Her nose was red and her eyes were puffy.

'I just don't understand why you do things like that, Caroline,' she said, and her voice sounded as if she had a bad cold.

Caroline said nothing. She didn't know, either. She pulled out a handful of her fine blonde hair. It hurt as she pulled it, but it made her feel better afterwards.

'Stop doing that,' said her mother. 'You'll be bald if you keep on doing that and how will you feel then?'

Bad, thought Caroline, but then I always feel bad.

'Mum,' she said again. 'Will you help me with my spellings?'

'I think I'd like to hear you say "sorry", first,' said her mother, sitting on the bed with a resigned air.

'Sorry,' said Caroline obediently.

'And you'll never let it happen again?'

Caroline nodded. 'I'll never let it happen again,' she repeated.

It was a lie and she knew it. It would happen again. And she would not be able to prevent it. Still tomorrow would be okay.

It wasn't, though.

She had to go to see the doctor. First the long wait in the waiting-room, uneasily leafing through an out-of-date copy of *Hello* magazine while her mother told the doctor all about what she was doing and then the doctor himself, kind, puzzled. The usual questions. Why did she do it? Was something upsetting her? And then back to the waiting-room again while there was another conference with her mother and then home, everyone being very carefully kind to her and watching her uneasily all the time. Homework. All the family falling over themselves to help her. False praise, false words of affection.

Three days of peace. Caroline began to breathe more easily. All the time at school when she wasn't writing, or pulling out her hair, she kept her fingers crossed under the table. If there is another three days, she thought to herself, it will never happen again. Twice times three is good luck, she thought, trying to persuade herself that she had heard that said.

Her mother had been in to see the headmistress; she knew that. She had seen her in the corridor, dodging behind the computer trolley. Caroline had pretended not to see her and afterwards she had seen the headmistress talking to her teacher and then her teacher had started talking to Caroline with that same special voice, praising her for nothing and taking no notice when Caroline was talking instead of doing her work. And the headmistress too. Telling her how much her mother loved her. Caroline cried and promised never to do those terrible things again.

But, that night, it started again.

And this time, it was serious.

Caroline was in her bedroom doing her homework; Maria and Philip were in their rooms doing theirs. Their mother had gone upstairs to get ready for going out to the pub, going out to show off her brand new husband to everyone else in the village. Suddenly there were screams and a terrible choking, acrid smell of burning cloth. A bright new scarlet dress, short, tight, as the fashion was, had been set on fire, right in the middle of the bed.

It did not take long to put out the fire. Even the bedclothes were not much spoiled; but, of course, the new dress was ruined. Maria, with a sidelong glance of reproach at Caroline, put the dress in the bin, hung the scorched blanket on the line and put the smoke-smelling sheets and pillow cases into the washing machine. Philip seemed, for once, too stunned to say anything. Caroline knew what he felt like. She felt stunned herself, numb, deadened, completely without feeling.

It was almost a relief when her mother lost her careful calm, her false sweetness and rushed at her, slapping her face, shouting at her. Caroline could hear her step-father saying, 'Ann, stop it. You know what the doctor said. She can't help it. We must be kind to her.' And then he was pulling her mother's hands away, holding her, and her mother was crying.

'You had better go to bed, Caroline,' said Maria, appearing with a cup of tea. 'Go to bed now. I don't know how you could do such a thing.'

Caroline obeyed silently, twisting her hair between her fingers and trying not to cry. She undressed and got into bed. She turned off the light and then got out of bed again and stole across the room and opened the door. Yes, she was right. Her mother had phoned her friend, a woman called Tracy, and she was telling her about it.

'We're going to try and get an urgent appointment with the child psychiatrist,' she said. 'This just can't go on. We are going to watch her for every minute of the day until something can be done. Maria and Philip are going to help, also. There will never be a time when Caroline is alone from now on.'

Caroline stole back into bed. She felt comforted. If she were being watched all the time, then these terrible things could not go on. They would just have to stop. She fell asleep and didn't dream, although, in the morning, there were handfuls of the pale blonde hair on the pillowslip.

'You're going bald,' said one of the girls in her class the next morning. 'I can see your scalp, all pink through your hair.'

'It's just the spring,' said Caroline. 'Blonde people always lose hair in the spring.'

She knew that a lot of the girls were staring at her. She didn't care. She quite liked it really, especially when her teacher stood behind her and stroked her hair gently and praised her handwriting. It wasn't particularly good handwriting but it was nice to be praised. Nice to be pitied. Nice to have people fond of you.

The visit to the child psychiatrist was more difficult, though. The woman kept peering at her and asking all sorts of strange questions, and, of course, over and over again the same old question: 'Why did you do it?'

'I didn't,' said Caroline, but she said it without any conviction. She knew that it was a bad answer, but she could only think of that, and of 'I don't know.'

For the rest of the afternoon, she alternated the two answers, but neither seemed to be satisfactory. Then she was put into a room all by herself and given dolls to play with, but that was just plain stupid. She was too old for dolls. She would be nine on her next birthday. She sat on the chair and put her head in her hands and fell asleep. When she woke up, she knew that her mother was in the next room. She could just hear her voice. Quickly she slipped over and opened the door. She could hear them now.

'Really, I have always found Caroline difficult,' her mother was saying. 'She was just so different from Maria. Maria was an enchanting baby and so clever too. She's so good at school, but poor little Caroline is very average, or even below average, at everything. But you know, in the past few months, before all this started, she had begun to improve quite a bit, both her looks and her school work. I remember saying to Maria that Caroline was going to turn into quite a pretty girl.'

There was a murmur from the child psychiatrist and then her mother's clear, carrying voice again.

'Well, we'll try that. I'll be glad to do anything possible. This sort of thing just can't go on. It's not fair to anyone.'

'I'll talk to her, then.' This was the psychiatrist's voice, and from the sound of it Caroline knew that she had got up and was walking towards the door. Quick as a flash, Caroline shut the door and went back to her chair.

'Well, Caroline,' the psychiatrist's voice was jolly. 'Sometimes children go through a phase of doing destructive things, but then they just grow out of it. Your mother tells me that you will be nine next week and I'm sure that it will never happen again after that.'

Only another week, thought Caroline as she listened to her mother telling Philip and Maria all about it when they got home. Maria looked a bit startled, she thought, and Philip said immediately:

'That's just ridiculous.'

'Hush,' said his mother quickly.

'Why do you think it's ridiculous?' asked Caroline following Philip into the dining room.

'Because it is,' he said rudely. 'You'll probably end up completely nutty and have to spend the rest of your days in the funny farm hearing sounds like these.'

He picked up one of her mother's tapes and began to run it at high speed on the tape recorder. Caroline ran out of the room. The high pitched squeaky sounds made her feel sick and she suddenly felt terrified.

The tape will break and then I'll be responsible, she thought as she quickly slipped into the kitchen.

'Can I stay with you, Mummy?' she asked.

'Yes,' said her mother, stopping in the middle of dialling a number and putting down the phone. 'Or perhaps Maria would help you with your homework.

Maria, Maria!' she called from the bottom of the stairs. 'Caroline is coming up to your room. Will you look after her?'

'Do you think it will stop when I'm nine, Maria?' asked Caroline as she sat on Maria's bed and looked at her hair in the mirror.

Maria looked at her seriously. No wonder Mummy liked her best, thought Caroline. She is the most beautiful person I have ever seen. She held her breath and waited to hear what Maria would say.

'Well, it might,' said Maria, but Caroline's heart sank when she heard the doubtful tone.

I'll just have to make sure that someone is with me all the time, she thought.

She slept badly and woke easily. She could hear footsteps outside her door. Was it Philip? It sounded like him. What was he doing? Was something going to happen? Panic-stricken, Caroline switched on her bedside light.

But it wasn't Philip; it was Maria. Caroline had switched on the light so quickly that Maria had no time to hide what she was doing. She had a painting in her hand, a painting of the lakes of Killarney which had been done after a school trip. Maria had won a prize for it. Now Maria had torn it across the middle — a big ugly tear right through the centre of the picture. Caroline looked at it and blinked. She felt confused. She couldn't understand. Maria spoke quickly, her voice slightly panicky:

'It was just a joke, Caroline; it was all just a joke, really. Don't tell anyone.'

As Caroline gazed at her big sister, she was conscious only of a feeling of great relief. So it hadn't been her after all. That was the only thing that seemed to matter. She looked at Maria, and for the second time that day, she asked:

'Maria, do you think all this destruction *will* stop when I am nine?'

This time there was not a shadow of doubt in Maria's voice. She looked straight at Caroline with her beautiful pale blue eyes and said steadily:

'I'm sure it will stop, Caroline. It will never happen again.'

Mark O'Sullivan is a writer whose work has received critical esteem from adults as well as popularity with its intended readership and frank envy from his peers. His book Melody For Nora *won the first Eilis Dillon Memorial Award in 1995, and was shortlisted for the Reading Association of Ireland Book Award in the same year, while* More Than a Match *was shortlisted for the 1997 Bisto Book of the Year Award. In 1998 he had two books -* White Lies *and* Angels Without Wings *- shortlisted for the same award, while* White Lies *was chosen for the White Ravens series by the International Youth Library.*

MUSIC FOR DANCING AND CRYING TO

by Mark O'Sullivan

They keep on asking me, are you alright, are you sure you're alright? They're driving me round the twist. Yeah, yeah, yeah. I'm grand, fine, no problem. What do they expect me to say? What do they expect me to do? Cry, wail, screech like a gull into their faces? I can just see it if I did. Me hegging into their shoulders and them looking around the room, afraid to put their hands on me, looking for someone to rescue them. At Mam maybe, who's quieter even than I am though she's talking all the time but no one can hear her except the person she's talking to and maybe even they can't, because the music never stops.

Polkas, slip jigs, reels. The room is full of famous people. Traditional musicians, rock stars, jazz heads, producers, film people. But my father, for tonight the most famous of them all, isn't knocking back the whiskey or shouting the crowd down with his laughing banter. And his button accordion, *the box*, is set up on a special table like an altar, with his fiddle and flute and his mandolin, and the tapes and c.d.'s he made.

Opened out in a long, winding curve the box is — like it's stuck in the middle of a tune. Every time I look at it, I'm thinking how the hell am I ever going to figure out anything now, after what he did to us. I'm thinking, everyone in this room loves him as he lies up there in Cloghercree graveyard. Even Mam. Even Joe Don't Say Much, who taught him more tunes than there are nights in a year to pass with music. And the worst thing is, they're all waiting for me to play. Like, if I play, that'll make everything okay. As if the music he gave me is bigger than the betrayal.

It's a big room, bigger than all the other rooms in the cottage it's attached to. You can't see the view now but, out of the dark, and simmering under the music and talk, you can feel the swell of the Atlantic and the waves foaming on the rocks of the cliff face. The ballroom, he called this place and I never liked it. Always swarming with visitors and people talking contracts and planning to take him away for yet another tour or recording session. I can just about remember life in the cottage when he was only well-known and we had him more or less to ourselves, most of the time. Or we thought we had.

There must be a hundred people in here and their glances are like an unrelenting rain beating in my face that's supposed to be so like his. I don't want to think about him but I can't stop. Thinking is the wrong word for it, anyway. More like a tune buzzing around in your head until you get it right on the box, make it live. Except it's a tune I don't want to make live. I want to destroy it but I can't. Like he said to me, one time, after hearing a major rock icon making a pig's ass of an old Irish air - *You can't kill a tune but, by Jaysus, you can murder it.* See, I can't even stop smiling at his jokes. After everything. After him dying in America, so far away we couldn't even say goodbye. If we had still wanted to.

The ballroom is sweltering but Mam keeps herself busy, keeping the fire going. My father always liked a fire to look into, even during the summer, never mind on cold, blustery November nights like this one. When Joe told us, she sat down from where she was gripping the edge of the kitchen table - What, Joe? - crumpling softly, her hands coming together in her lap like she was closing a book. I'll miss him, she said, I'll miss him terrible. Each time, after she drops another sod of turf on the fire, her hands join together in that way and I'm reminded of what flashed through my mind when Joe Don't Say Much spoke. How much I hated my father and, for a split second, how glad I was that he'd died.

I have to get out of this room or I'll crack up with the music and all those eyes on me and my eyes on Mam's hands, and the ocean whispering outside and the gulls calling at me. I make it over to the door without having my hand shaken or anyone saying, 'Sorry, man' or 'I can't believe he's gone.' I know if I find any of those famous faces hovering around the cottage I'll freak out and tell them to stay in the ballroom because that was his and this is ours, Mam's and mine. But no one's there and I head into the kitchen where the table's littered with half-full, half-empty bottles of whiskey, brandy, gin, vodka and I think about trying something, trying everything, a swig out of every bottle.

Then I see the picture of him on the wall by the dresser. A close-up, his lean face glows a soft red-gold out of a dark background. A state of grace, Mam called that look. Not a big wide-grinned happiness or a grimace of tormented sainthood. There's the ghost of a smile and the eyes looking towards the camera though you know it's something inside himself he's looking at.

I remember him coming back from recording some T.V. programme in a pub in Tipperary. Not falling down drunk or anything, he was never like that, but nicely as he'd say himself. And he said:

There was this crowd and they were concentrating so hard on playing every note exactly right and the constipated faces on them, you'd imagine they were sitting on the jacks. One tune after another and no more style than an ould dog wandering down the street and lifting his leg at every lamp post. I felt like roaring, Whatever ye do, don't enjoy yourselves anyway, for fear ye'd break yere stride.

That time, he was only half-way between being well-known and famous. No matter what part of Ireland he played in, he'd come home every night. Sometimes it would be getting light over at the cliffs when he'd make it back. But you can't come back from America for the night. All the way across the Atlantic Ocean that's beckoning to me louder than ever in the kitchen quiet. And why would you come anyway, when you had another woman over there to stay with, to hold your hand when you were dying? Looking at the bottles again. The way the low kitchen light makes all that gold and silvery alcohol seem so innocent. As if it was okay as long as it didn't turn you into a monster, only a long, red-faced, laugh-a-minute trickster like my father was. As if the drink wasn't a river that couldn't be crossed between where we lived and where he lived in his head.

Someone's shuffling along the hallway and I wish to

God it was him, so I could tell him what I think of him. But it can't ever be him again and whoever it is, I swear I'll scream at them. But it's only Joe Don't Say Much.

Joe's in his seventies, has a shell-white beard and a bush of hair that, my father used to say, *would collapse in a heap if it ever felt the prod of a brush.* His nickname comes from his wife's description of his legendary quietness — 'Joe don't say much.' He's tight with money. He's lived long enough to inherit four farms, and dresses like a man of the road. With everything else he's generous — tunes, nods of encouragement, his time. No one ever heard him say a bad word about anyone. Bad words about my father are what I want to hear now.

'How can she forgive him so easily, Joe?'

Joe plays the box with a cigarette dangling from the corner of his mouth, his left eye half-closed to the smoke. He's played so many tunes down the years, his eyelid's in a permanent droop and he always looks like he's sizing you up. He even talks sideways as if there's an invisible cigarette in his mouth when he's not smoking.

'I wouldn't say it was easy.'

'And what about you? He ripped off your tunes and he copied your style.'

'I only passed on the tunes. He had his own way with them.'

'You taught him everything he knew.'

'I did but, sure, playing isn't what you know, it's what you can do.'

We're both staring at the picture on the wall now. Outside, the wind is getting up, turning up the sea's hissing volume and the gulls' interfering squawks — daring me. Joe lights a cigarette and I see the flare-up of the match reflected on the framed glass. The flash sets me thinking again like it's lighting up a different part of my brain. I'm adding things up I never added up before, things he said.

Whatever you do, don't get married until you're thirty. And, *I never set foot outside Ireland until I was thirty.* And, *You can't wait for the world to come to you, you have to go out into it, like my granduncle says - the lad I met in Australia last year - you can't sell your cattle if you don't go to the mart.* And, *When I'm on the road, I'm a different man.*

I'm adding these things up but I'm not getting a clear answer except all the stuff I thought was advice was just him preparing me for what was coming.

He's thirty in that photo. It's on the cover of the c.d. that started it all for him. *Ceol Damhsa agus Caointe* — Music for Dancing and Crying To. After that, everyone wanted a piece of him. Last year, when he came back from America for the third time in six months, he spent a long time telling me where the title came from and what it meant. I thought he was telling me something about the secret of music-making but it was just more preparation for the big let-down. Last year, when he was already seeing the woman who was there when his heart gave out. Thinking about her, about *their* little secret, makes me feel sick. If I drink some of this stuff on the kitchen table, maybe it'll take the taste out of my mouth.

I'm breaking up, losing the tune, or as he'd say, *losing the run of meself.* Joe Don't Say Much knows, though he's still looking at the picture on the wall. I'm ready to reach for the nearest bottle and he says:

'Leave the drink awhile.'

'What am I going to do, Joe?'

'You don't need me to tell you.'

It doesn't seem like much of an answer as he leaves the kitchen. Just me now, and that famous face up on the wall, a face shining like some kind of impossible midnight sun. Still looking through me as if I'm the one who doesn't exist any more and not him.

Will you, for once in your life or your death or whatever, will you look at me when I'm talking to you? This is what you left. To everyone else, the music and the laughs to remember. To Mam, the unfair task of forgiveness. To me, you left a half-brother or a half-sister waiting to be born in America and, like me, with nothing for a father except a face on the cover of a c.d. You can keep the rest. I don't want your music and I'll prove it to you. That's what the ocean is telling me to do and the gulls. Prove it. Prove it.

I wait until I hear Joe Don't Say Much open the ballroom door, letting out a sharp gust of roaring talk and closing it off behind him. Along the hallway to my bedroom, I don't have to think any more because it's all decided. I take down my copy of *Ceol Damhsa agus Caointe* from the rack and pocket it. From under the bed I pull out the accordion, the one he learned from Joe on, the one I learned from him on, the pearl red Hohner.

At the back door, the wind tries to bully me back inside but I'm stronger and I face it down. Clouds race each other across the moon. The hair whips across my face, but I can see the path winding upwards along the cliff edge. He's talking to me and I'm not listening, only telling him to shut up. Actually saying it like a madman out for a midnight ramble and arguing with the voices inside his mad head. Shut up. Shut up.

I'm twelve years old again. I'm following him up the path. In the cottage, he was teaching me a reel and I said I couldn't play that fast, it hurt my arms too much and my fingers.

Come on, we'll go walking and you'll keep up with me. Come on, you little fecker, you're nearly as tall as me already. Stride for stride, keep up with me. An ould lad like me and you can't — good man, that's it. We're like soldiers now. Left, right, left, right. Marching through the pain, a grand, even pace all the way to the top. That's the job. See, if anyone saw us walking up here now they'd be thinking, there's a grand easy slope to walk up because we make it look easy but it isn't, is it? And the music's the same. Once you don't mind it hurting, you can do anything and make it look easy.

Shut up. Shut up. I'm not even half-way there and the accordion's made of lead and the edge of the c.d. cover is scraping the flesh on my thigh. *Ceol Damhsa agus Caointe.* Music for Dancing and Crying To. And he's off again, talking, spoofing, his whiskey breath is everywhere on the wind. Shut up. Shut up.

Music was made, from day one, for two things - dancing and crying to. And the secret, my secret any-way, is to play the dances, the jigs, the reels, like you're crying inside. And to play the laments and the slow airs like you're laughing inside. Because. Will I tell you the because?

Shut up. Shut up.

Because life is funny sad and death is a cruel joke.

Shut up. Shut up. I'm near the top of the rise. The wind is blowing all the way from America. Ninety, a hundred feet above the waves, I feel the mist of spray on my face. I hear the gulls crying like children, like new-born babies, but I don't see them. Shut up. Shut up. And he's talking again. His voice is softer, so soft that if he was really here and not just in my head, I wouldn't hear him at all.

When you're losing the run of yourself, when you're fit to be tied, go out to the cliffs and scream your head off into the wind until the gulls take up your tune and then learn it back off them.

Shut up. Shut up. I'm there. The top of the rise, where the cliff juts out like a big ugly granite chin. I swing the accordion back and forward. Counting like for the start of a tune. One. Two. Three. Four. And I let it go. I don't see it disappear because my hair lashes stripes of burning ice across the balls of my eyes. I fish the c.d. case out of my pocket and get the disc out. I take a last look at the photo of him on the cover and I toss the plastic case over the side. The moon makes a strange rainbow-coloured cross on the c.d.'s silver surface and I spin it away. The wind draws it up. A UFO. An Unwanted Flying Object and, for once, I laugh at one of my own cruel jokes and not one of his. But the wind can't hold it for long and when the disc goes down it goes down like a tossed coin.

I start to scream. No words to it. No notes to it. Only stopping to get the breath to scream again and hear the gulls screaming back at me. Screaming until I can't remember if the screaming started with me or with them. Screaming until it feels like I'm doing the screaming for all of them — Mam, Joe Don't Say Much, the woman in America, the unborn child, my father. Screaming until I can't scream any more.

I seem to be floating now. Down the cliff path, down towards that little point of light, the cottage ballroom. That little point of light, multiplying itself, taking shape. Shapes forming within the shapes. My mother and Joe standing at the back-lit door. There's some kind of smile on my face, I know, because she smiles back at me and it's the first time since she told me that things had changed between them and he wouldn't be coming back from America. She brushes a hand through my wild and damp hair and she says:

'You're wet to the skin. I missed you.'

She slips back into the warm cottage and Joe holds the door open for me. The wind is pushing at my back and blowing Joe's hair around like a clump of dead grass. I don't know why I'm laughing.

'Tell us, Joe, have I the same mad head on me as you do?'

'Couldn't say. I never look in the mirror. Bad luck that.'

'I'm mad, Joe, I'm gone mad.'

'Deed and you're not. Come on inside and we'll rise 'em out of it.'

'I threw 'way the box, Joe.'

'That's alright, there's a spare one inside.'

I follow Joe into the cottage and through the crowded ballroom to the table, the altar. When I pick up my father's accordion, the Paolo Morini - all timber and whorled grains - there's a big breathy sigh out of it I can hear because things are going dead quiet like a wave going out. I go and sit beside my mother and Joe sits at the other side of the fireplace. I watch his foot, the old boot muddy as ever.

My father and Joe Don't Say Much always started off with the same old joke. Looking down at Joe's tapping foot, the crumbs of dried clay dropping off of it, my father would say fast to the count of a quick three: *Wouldn't you buy yourself a pair of shoes and you having three farms?* Four, Joe laughs, and we're off.

I play the crying out of it.   I play the hell out of it.
We play dancing into it.
We play heaven into it.

Autograph Album

The rest of the material in Big Pictures is about Lucan Educate Together National School, and may be of more interest to adults. But we thought we'd leave you with one last thing, and so far as we know it's the first time it's been done.

So this bit is for the very many people who like collecting autographs. You won't need me to tell you how popular a pastime it is — if you don't yet collect them yourself, you probably have friends who do. All of our contributors make personal appearances all over Ireland, and they get lots of requests for autographs, both in the post and while they're visiting schools and libraries. They sign autograph albums, copies of their books, and pieces of paper of every size and description.

For those who would like to collect the autographs of our contributors (you may well have some of them already!), we thought we'd give you a place to keep them all together, making your copy of *Big Pictures* a very special one. Maybe they'll be visiting your school, or appearing at your local bookshop or library. If so, bring along your copy of the book and demand a signature — it's free! But you can also contact any of them by writing to them care of their publishers. If you've wanted to do that, but have never bothered because you didn't think you'd get a reply, then have a go — you might be surprised.

Marie-Louise Fitzpatrick (Dublin):

Maeve Friel (Dublin):

Cora Harrison (Clare):

John Leonard (Dublin and Armagh):

Morgan Llywelyn (Dublin):

P.J. Lynch (Dublin):

Liam Mac Uistin (Meath):

Frank Murphy (Cork):

Aislinn O'Loughlin (Dublin):

Larry O'Loughlin (Dublin):

Mark O'Sullivan (Tipperary):

Siobhán Parkinson (Dublin):

Michael Scott (Dublin):

Carolyn Swift (Dublin):

Marilyn Taylor (Dublin):

Gerard Whelan (Dublin):

Well, that's about it from the story part of Big Pictures. Thank you for reading our book, and I hope you found something you liked in it. If you need any more copies, or know someone who'd like one but can't find a copy in the bookshop, there's an order form at the end. So long, and enjoy yourself. Keep reading!

LETS and Educate Together

THE SCHOOL OF STORY

When they ask locally where our school is sited in Lucan, the directions often given are 'down by the Liffey, halfway up the hill, somewhere in the woods'. And sure enough there it is, by the meandering water: halfway up the hill, where up meets down and down meets up, among the great trees. In the middle of that fertile crescent, that river basin, that rich alluvial soil – a place fit to fire a Joyce, a Heaney, even a Sweeney.

The water, the clay and the wood – just think what they have seen! They are ancient witnesses to, and keepers of, a whole universe of stories. A perfect place to listen to stories, really: to collect them. What better place, then, to start a school – a shrine from which many children will embark on their own individual voyages of discovery?

Story – particularly this collection of stories, with its unique connection to our school – is a most profound gift. It will enrich that voyage of discovery for many children. This collection has been made and given to us here in our school; we, in our turn, do what you are supposed to do with stories: we pass it on, not just to our own pupils but to children we will never see. It's what stories are for; it's what education is for. Education is a story.

Collections like this bring us back to the source, the fountainhead of all knowledge – to the 'fifth province' of Ireland. That province is Story; and Story, as the word implies, stores many things for us – as individuals, as communities, and as a nation composed of both these entities. It helps us attend to our inner, imaginative life, and gives the soul the nourishment it needs to grow. Stories, told and retold to children by grandparents, parents and teachers, enrich those depths of soul from which later hopes and ideals are born.

'The story motifs are absorbed by millions of souls during their formative years…and no other creation has such a fundamental effect on generations of people.' So wrote Rudolf Meyer in his book *The Wisdom of Fairytales*.

'Is that story true?' a group of Irish schoolchildren asked intently as Skyhorse, a Lakota Sioux Indian, finished one of his tales.

'It may or it may not be,' he assured them. 'But inside every story there are many truths.'

In the Curriculum of the Soul, story and meaningful ritual are the pillar posts of the Gates of the Kingdom. In a time of reason and ever-increasing technology, the unique collection of stories that is *Big Pictures* opens the gates to the Kingdom of Story. That such a diversity of style and content can be held in a single volume is indeed a metaphor for an Educate Together school that holds diversity at its very core.

The writers and illustrators who have contributed to this work are all celebrated in their field. We thank each of them equally, and with genuine sincerity – not just for their contributions, but for being who they are and doing what they do. They are the ones who know the topography of the Kingdom of Story; we can only share with them the sense of excitement on a voyage that is always one of discovery. We thank them for helping us all to mark again the co-ordinates of that fifth province, and for cultivating and nourishing the curriculum of the soul in a climate which incubates many educational viruses.

Schools, like this book, are brimful of stories. In Lucan Educate Together School we listen to them. It is the very least we can do: to open the gates even a little, and listen with reverence and respect. Maybe then we can encompass what education really involves – the dialogue of Story and the Soul.

Soon our own school will acquire a new site – a permanent home. It will grow larger, more sophisticated, and even more complicated. We would do well to remember then the story of how it all began – to revisit the source, near the Liffey, halfway up the hill, somewhere in the woods. Where up meets down and down meets up. As with each life, so with each school: it's as well to keep sight of the Big Pictures.

Tom Conaty
Principal
Lucan Educate Together National School

ABOUT LUCAN EDUCATE TOGETHER SCHOOL

For us it all started in February 1997, when local residents' associations in the Lucan area called a public meeting to make people aware of the Educate Together option in education. Lucan was reported to be the fastest growing suburb in Europe, and school places were at a premium: people listened.

The Educate Together idea was simple: educate our children in an all-inclusive environment, with respect for all irrespective of gender, religion, physical ability or ethnic background. Where all children are cherished.

Sounds easy? The catch is that you have to do most of the work yourself — YOU, the parents.

A small group was charged to see whether founding an E.T. school in Lucan was feasible: did enough people want it? An open pre-enrolment day was planned to test the waters. Invitations to enrol in the school were sent out to residents and residents' associations, and early one Saturday morning enrolment began. A queue had formed before the doors even opened, and the day was a great success. This seemed to answer our question.

The first AGM of Lucan Educate Together School (then known as Lucan Multidenominational School) was called, and the first Executive Committee elected.

The application to the Department of Education was lodged and work started on finding temporary premises. The Scouts in Lucan welcomed us as tenants of their Den, and planning permission was sought for change of use. But by then time was running out for the start of the school year in September, and frantic work began to make the building suitable for the thirty-two pupils who'd start on September first. A dedicated group of parents, committee members - and people who just thought it was a good idea - started work on the new school.

After a rather stressful summer, Lucan Educate Together NS opened its doors to children on September first, 1997. The school was positioned between St Mary's Catholic boys school (at the bottom of Chapel Hill) and St Mark's Church of Ireland school (at the top). Hidden behind a picturesque wood in the Liffey valley, we had our school: it was a reality. Principal Tom Conaty and assistant Sereen McCormack began teaching the children using the Educate Together ideals: co-educational, democratic, child-centred and multidenominational.

From the first it was wonderful to see the children develop a love for their school and their classmates. Sereen worked with the infant class till the end of the first term when a permanent appointment, Fionnuala McHugh, was made. At the end of the second term - Christmas in the Christian tradition - the children staged a concert, with the senior classes putting on an imaginative play incorporating a multitude of religious stories.

In early 1998 Lucan Educate Together School was

incorporated and became a legal entity. The school had its official opening day, attended by the Italian Ambassador's wife. A fax was received from President Mary McAleese, wishing the school well. Now it's late 1998, and the way things are going we'll grow out of our home in the Scouts den: the school that started with 32 students and parents' sweat will now, a year later, have tripled our student number.

And next year? Who knows. It's another year.

I am very proud to be part of this very active and vibrant community, dedicated to the education of children in an environment which promotes difference and teaches tolerance. Where every child is special and where every culture accepted and cherished. It is a very special school in a very special time in Ireland.

Seán Murphy
Chairperson, Executive Committee, LETS
Website: http://ireland.iol.ie/~mdslucan
Email: mdslucan@iol

ABOUT EDUCATE TOGETHER

Lucan Educate Together National School is one of almost twenty National Schools operating in the Republic of Ireland that offer a unique type of education for children at primary level.

Historically in Ireland, both North and South, children have been segregated along denominational lines during the formative years of their early school days. Many parents feel that such an education is no longer appropriate for children growing up as part of an Irish society of ever-increasing diversity and as citizens of a small planet with instant global communication and cross-cultural interaction.

As a result, the concept of the Educate Together school was born. Each individual school has come into being as a response to parental demand and as a result of the hard work and dedication of the parents, teachers and other supporters involved, who come together to form a voluntary and charitable support Association that also acts as the Patron of the school.

All Educate Together schools subscribe to the Educate Together Charter, which lays down the principles that inform the characteristic spirit of the schools. That is, that they shall be:

— Multi-denominational i.e. all children having equal rights of access to the school, and children of all social, cultural and religious backgrounds being equally respected.

— Co-educational and committed to encouraging all children to explore their full range of abilities and opportunities.

— Child-centred in their approach to education.

— Democratically run with active participation by parents in the daily life of the school, with due regard however for the professional role of the teachers.

For many years, the schools in the Educate Together sector have struggled to survive under very difficult financial circumstances. This has been due to the less favourable funding arrangements offered by the State compared to other school types, and to the requirement for parents to purchase sites for the school buildings, and to contribute substantial sums to the cost of school construction.

As a result, all Educate Together schools have had to open in temporary premises, that are often far from ideal for the purpose of running a school. The financial and other difficulties that parents have had to face to secure an Educate Together education for their child are only now beginning to be recognised by the State, and the lack of adequate state support for the development of the sector through its national organisation is still a severe handicap.

Lucan Educate Together School, as a fledgling school in its second year of operation, is in a particularly vulnerable financial situation, and the generosity of the authors and others who have contributed to this publication is greatly appreciated. It is particularly appropriate that such an educational and child-centred method of fund-raising has been adopted by an Educate Together school.

I would like to congratulate all involved in the production of this lovely book, and wish the school every success in the future.

Jill Steer
Chairperson, Educate Together

For further information contact Educate Together at:
9B John Player House,
276/278 South Circular Road,
Dublin 8.
Tel: 353 1 473 0309
Fax: 353 1 472 0286
Website at: http://www.educatetogether.ie
Email: info@educatetogether.ie

Educate Together Schools in the Republic of Ireland 1998/9

Bray School Project
Killarney Road
Ballywaltrim
Bray
Co. Wicklow
Tel: 01 - 286 4242

Cork School Project
Grattan Street
Cork
Tel: 021 - 275 640

Dalkey School Project
Glenageary Lodge
Glenageary
Co. Dublin
Tel: 01 - 285 7199

Ennis School Project
Gort Road
Ennis
Co. Clare
Tel: 065 - 628 0070

Gaelscoil an Ghoirt Alainn
Bóthar Gleann Maghir Meanach
Montenotte
Corcaigh
Tel: 021 - 509 072

Galway School Project
Corrib Village
Newcastle Road
Galway
Tel: 091 - 278 87

Griffith Barracks National School
S.C.R.
Dublin 8
Tel: 01 - 454 7278

Kilkenny School Project
Springfield
Waterford Road
Kilkenny
Tel: 056 - 514 07

Limerick School Project
O'Connell Avenue
Limerick
Tel: 061 - 412 994

Lucan Educate Together National School
Chapel Hill
Lucan
Co. Dublin
Tel: 01 - 628 1298

Monkstown Educate Together National School
Monkstown Grove
Dún Laoghaire
Co. Dublin
Tel: 01 - 280 4426

North Bay National School Project
Greendale Avenue
Dublin 5
Tel: 01 - 832 5536

North Dublin National School Project
Church Avenue
Dublin 9
Tel: 01 - 837 1620

North Kildare Project School
Clane Road
Ballymakealy
Celbridge
Co. Kildare
Tel: 01 - 627 4388